"Who are you?"
Donna demanded

He leaned against the bulkhead, and the sea's reflection danced over his face. "I've told you my name—Brent Sanders. What more do you want to know?"

"Is this how you make your living?" She indicated the underwater photos of the wreck.

"No. It's a hobby." He smiled. "You should learn to hide your contempt better. Not everyone outside your charmed circle is a peasant, Donna." He nodded as he saw her expression. "I see you understand."

"I didn't mean—"

"Oh, but you did. You may be sick of your world, but you still possess the arrogant superiority of your kind." He swept the photos together. "I could tell you more, but I won't. I feel no need to impress you. You know enough for now."

Books by Mary Wibberley

HARLEQUIN ROMANCES

HARLEQUIN PRESENTS

These books may be available at your local bookseller.

For a free catalog listing of all titles currently available, send your name and address to:

Harlequin Reader Service
P.O. Box 52040, Phoenix, AZ 85072-2040
Canadian address: P.O. Box 2800, Postal Station A,
5170 Yonge St., Willowdale, Ont. M2N 5T5

Golden Haven

Mary Wibberley

Harlequin Books

TORONTO • NEW YORK • LONDON
AMSTERDAM • PARIS • SYDNEY • HAMBURG
STOCKHOLM • ATHENS • TOKYO • MILAN

Original hardcover edition published in 1984
by Mills & Boon Limited

ISBN 0-373-02664-1

Harlequin Romance first edition December 1984

CHAPTER ONE

THE island was waiting for her. Donna Webster looked down from the cockpit of her small seaplane, and there it was, a lush green triangle surrounded by golden sands, with hidden inlets and bays. Paradise Island, an uninhabited member of the Windwards at the eastern side of the Caribbean Sea, is perhaps aptly named—perhaps not. She didn't seek paradise but peace—namely of mind, and here, alone for the next few days or even weeks, she hoped to find it.

Her mind was finely attuned to her task now, no time for thoughts of what had brought her here, only the concentration needed to make a perfect landing. Donna, at twenty-three, had been a qualified pilot for four years, and was as accomplished in this as she was in everything else she did. She was a winner, in everything. It was one of the many reasons she had had to get away. One of a great many, but not the most important. . . .

She circled the island, choosing her spot with care, going lower, lower until the green blur resolved into individual trees, tall feathery palms stirring in a slight breeze, shrubs with colourful profusions of flowers; poinsettias a flash of bright scarlet and pink against the green, and long clusters of ferns nearer the sands. Towards the higher part and in the centre of the island were rocks, huge grey-brown slabs rising from the ground, and between them the freshwater spring that welled from somewhere deep in the earth to fall down the hillside in a never-ending waterfall of crystal that sparkled like diamonds in the afternoon sun.

Donna took a deep breath. Nonie had described it accurately, even though she had not been for years. Her memory was as keen as her perception. She had known why Donna had gone to her, even before it had all come pouring out. She had known, but she had waited to be told all the same, and in the telling of it had come some measure of relief for Donna.

Lower, lower, until she was practically skimming the white-crested waves, and nearing the place that she had chosen, a wide inlet virtually screened by trees where her seaplane would be safe and sheltered. Bump, bump, bump, the floats touched, bounced slightly, and she held tightly to the joystick as the little plane slowed and veered to the left, then she was coasting along, guiding it like a boat now, to port, and smooth, smoother into the green shade, and slow, slower, then almost to a halt and rocking gently, bobbing on the waves.

It was then, for the first time, that she saw the boat. It was a sleek white cabin cruiser moored ahead of her, and the reason she hadn't seen it before was because the trees had effectively provided a screen from above. She felt a sudden flash of anger, irrational and quickly controlled. She had come here to be alone. Nonie had been quite positive that *nobody* had been to Paradise Island for years. It was after all one of many islands too small to be mapped, that dotted the Caribbean. 'Damn, oh, damn,' she muttered, and for a moment wasn't concentrating, then her hand moved fractionally on the joystick, and she heard a screeching sound so faint as to be almost unheard, but she *felt* it as well, and a thread of fear touched her spine.

She switched off motors and fuel, unbuckled her belt and jumped down on a float to examine what damage, if any, had been done. There appeared nothing amiss. Pulling herself lithely up again, and into the plane, she began to stow her luggage near the door, ready for going ashore, and fifteen minutes later she was on the beach, ready to look round—and see who was there. She had come to be alone, and not with company. If the people already there were here for a while, then Donna would leave. There were other islands nearby. It would be quite simple to find one suitable—provided there was a supply of fresh water, as here.

She opened a can of Coke, drank it, then set off to explore. Paradise Island was truly beautiful; she could see that immediately. Birds sang in the trees nearby, the air had a faint sweet scent, and there was ample shelter from the blazing sun. She cupped her hands and called: 'Hello—anyone there?' and the faint echoes reverberated before vanishing. There was no reply, only the renewed chatter of the birds, as they began again after a brief, shocked silence. For an absurd moment, her heart lifted. Perhaps there was no one there. Perhaps the boat was an abandoned one. She looked round at it, and her heart sank again. Not much chance of that. It was brand spanking new, the paint white and gleaming, brass rails barely weathered. The name *Searcher II* was painted boldly on the stern in black and gold. On an impulse Donna went towards it, climbed up the short ladder and clambered on deck.

It was a large boat, sleek lines, luxurious, and the companionway which led to several cabins was at her left. She walked down slowly, and the boat rocked with her movement. At the bottom of the steps she stood for a moment and counted. Six doors, three either side—but not a whisper of sound. The first door on her right was open. She peeped in; a man lay stretched out on a bed, and Donna felt her heart stop for a second in sudden fear as she stared at him. He was a big man, and he lay across the bed at an angle, as though it wasn't quite long enough for him—which it obviously wasn't, for he was very tall, that much she took in at the first shocked impression. The other impressions followed almost immediately. He was clad only in blue cotton shorts, nothing else, and his body was tanned, hard, and even though relaxed, very muscular—and hairy. There was nothing gentle about his face even in repose. Hard, unshaven, a large straight nose, a wide mouth, slightly open, eyes dark-lashed, brows thick. His hair was black, flecked with grey, shaggy and overlong. He looked a very disreputable character indeed and her immediate impulse was to walk out, load up her plane and get as far away as possible. Without a sound she turned and crept out, towards the deck—only she never reached it. There was a flurry of sound, a rushing, roaring in her ears, and she was spun round to face the now awakened—and furious-looking-giant.

'What the devil!' he blazed, and Donna screamed with the shock.

He released her abruptly, and glowered down at her. 'Who the devil are *you*?' he asked, and he wanted an answer.

'I——' For a moment she was lost for words, which was ridiculous. She was *never* lost for words, only now, for the first time ever, she couldn't speak. She took a deep breath. 'I called,' she managed at last, fast regaining her control. 'I called out when I arrived——'

'You *did*?' he cut in, with heavy sarcasm. 'And when no one answered you came noseying round my boat——'

'I thought it was abandoned!' she snapped. One thing was sure, she could do without people like him in her life. Her first feelings of shock were vanishing fast. She didn't like his tone, his manner, and she certainly didn't like the look of him, a dislike strengthened at his roar of laughter which stopped her words.

'Abandoned? Does it look abandoned?' he asked. 'You'll have to do better than that. Who sent you?'

She stared at him. What on earth did he mean? 'Who sent you?' as if he was a criminal or something— she checked herself. That was ridiculous. If she let her imagination run riot she'd become frightened. Her one thought now was to leave here, with dignity if possible, but certainly with speed.

'No one sent me,' she responded, icily angry now. 'I flew here expecting a few days' peace and quiet. I didn't know you'd be here. I'm not very pleased either, if you really want to know.' She gave him a look that had effectively withered grown men before, only it didn't seem to do much to him, one way or the other. He narrowed his eyes.

'Flew?' he enquired. 'Alone?'

'Yes, alone. Ever heard of Amy Johnson? She did as well, and that was quite some time ago. And now, if you'll excuse me,' she paused, half turned away, and began to walk up the steps, 'I'm leaving. I have no wish to stay here with anyone—especially not *you*.'

She'd reached the deck before he took hold of her arm. 'I don't think so,' he said soft-voiced. 'Not yet anyway——'

She tried to shake her arm free. No one had ever dared to do that to her before, hold her, stop her. No one treated any of the Webster clan with anything but the greatest respect and deference. She was used to it. This was so surprising that it was almost like an assault. She turned and took hold of the hand that held her arm, and tried to prise it free. 'Take your hand away at *once*!' she demanded furiously.

He did so, almost with an air of amusement. 'You're not really in any position to give me orders,' he said to her, watching her, taking in every detail of her appearance in a way that was very obvious to Donna. It was almost an insolent summing up—and he looked as if he wasn't too pleased, and maybe faintly puzzled, at what he saw. 'You erupt into my life, waken me up from my siesta, trespass on my boat, and then think you can just up and leave the moment you choose. Well, I'm here to tell you that you can't. Before I decide whether you can go I want to know who you are and precisely why you're here.'

'I've already told you why. I'm here for a short holiday—alone.' She met his dark grey eyes fearlessly. The moments of fear had been brief; Donna was very capable of looking after herself. 'And as for my name, that's really none of your business.'

'Isn't it now? We'll see.' He gave a slight smile, a mere twitching of his large mouth. 'You're very sure of yourself.'

'I have no reason not to be.'

'You're alone. You expected—so you say—to be alone here, but instead you find me here—I could be a murderer, a rapist—anything you care to name——'

'And are you?'

'No.' He shook his head, and this time he smiled

properly; he had good teeth, and the smile reached his eyes—but he was laughing inwardly at her, and she didn't like that either. She didn't like him at all. 'I'm not. But I think you know what I am, don't you?'

'I haven't a clue.' Her shrug indicated that she didn't give a damn, and didn't want to know either.

He went very still, and the smile vanished. 'I don't believe you,' he answered softly.

'I don't care,' said Donna, equally soft. 'I'm going.'

'No, you're not.'

'Are you going to stop me?' She had shown fear once, when she had screamed. She wouldn't make that mistake again.

'Yes.'

'I see. By force, of course?' Her tone dripped acid contempt.

'If necessary. Why don't you tell me who you are?'

'I'm damned if I will. Who are *you*?'

'Brent Sanders—but I suspect you already know that.'

'I've never heard of you,' she answered. 'Are you supposed to be famous or something?'

'No. You'd better get down below, it's hot up here. We'll have a drink, then we'll talk.'

'I've nothing to say,' said Donna obstinately.

'You will have,' he smiled.

'Mr Sanders, I'll speak frankly. I don't like you, or your manner, or your questions. I've obviously made a mistake coming here—I accept that. You, after all, were here first. I have no intention of staying to be interrogated by you or anyone else here, I hope I make myself clear?'

'Perfectly. And I'm alone, just in case you'd wondered, and hadn't finished your search of my boat, and didn't like to ask—though I'm quite sure you're not frightened to ask anything you want to. And while you don't like me—perhaps with good reason—I don't accept that your arrival here is a mistake in your part. I don't believe in coincidences like that. This island is one of hundreds. I've been alone and undisturbed here for a full week, and not seen a soul, and that's entirely what I expected. I don't think anyone has been here for years. Yet lo, no sooner am I settled in than you fly in like a bird from out the blue—and express astonishment at my presence! Madam, you aren't half as astonished as I am.'

He was different, awake. The difference wasn't, alas, an improvement. He merely looked bigger, tougher, and even more intimidating. Donna was wearying of this battle of words. She was tired after her journey, and the shock of his presence was making itself felt.

'I've told you the truth,' she said. 'And I'm tired, and hot, and thirsty. I can't help it if you don't believe me.'

'Let's go to the galley and have a drink,' he suggested. 'I've a fridge full of iced beer.'

She was tempted. The temptation was almost overwhelming. Iced beer. Iced—in a frosty glass! Her parched throat protested the agony of waiting. 'I—have no wish to go there with you,' she said.

He lifted an amused eyebrow. 'You don't have much choice,' he answered bluntly. 'Think I'm going to go and fetch it while you get the hell out of here?' He shook his head, more, it seemed, in sorrow than in anger. 'Dear me, no!'

'I'm not stupid either,' she snapped. 'I'm not going there with *you*!'

'In case I attack you? Don't you know we're alone here? If I was in the mood for a quick rape, there's nothing to stop me here and now. No one is going to hear you scream—no one. Now, if you want a glass of iced beer you can come into the galley for it—you'll be as safe there as you are here.'

It was true. However coarse his words, and she sensed he had used them deliberately, she was in no more danger inside the boat than on deck. She wore jeans and thin sun-top. In the back pocket of her jeans she carried a small metal comb. That was the only weapon she had on her, but she had read enough to know how to defend herself. She stroked her hip, as if rubbing an irritation, felt the comb, and eased it out. He couldn't see, it was a back pocket, and she faced him still. With the comb concealed in her palm she nodded. 'All right.'

He turned and led the way past his cabin, to the door at the end of the passage. The galley was small, modern, well equipped. Cupboards and table and chairs bolted to the floor, and a cooker and a large refrigerator and sink.

'Sit down,' he said, and Donna obeyed. She rested the comb on the table beneath her left hand. Brent Sanders poured out two beers, foaming and icy, into two glasses, and handed her one.

'Thank you.' She took it and began to drink. Oh, it was nectar! As she did so, he leaned over and flipped up her left hand, revealing the comb. He took a deep swallow of beer, wiped the foaming moustache from his upper lip, and burst out laughing, a glorious deep-throated laugh. As Donna spluttered her indignation at his cavalier act, he said:

'I wondered what you were hiding. That's for me, is

it? He ran a finger under his nose and clicked his teeth. 'Guaranteed to bring tears to my eyes and give you time, no doubt, to make your escape.' He shook his head. 'A good idea. Do I really look so intimidating?'

'You're far from reassuring,' she responded.

'I'm not going to touch you—for God's sake, what do I have to do to make you believe that? I've no taste for fighting women. Just because I haven't shaved for a couple of days it doesn't make me a brute——'

'You've threatened me!' she retorted. 'You said you'd keep me here by force——'

'I'd prevent you going, yes. It was you who mentioned force, not me, remember? That doesn't mean I'd hurt you physically. There are ways of restraining people without hurting——' He paused to finish his glass of beer, and put the glass down. 'Drink up. This conversation is getting us nowhere fast. Just tell me who you are, who told you to come here, and why, and then I'll decide what to do about you.'

'What do you mean?'

'I can check up on you, that's what I mean. I've got a radio here. If you're who you say you are, if your reason for being here is genuine, and not what I suspect, I may let you go.'

Donna went suddenly cold. Only Aunt Nonie knew, and that was only for emergency use. She had made her promise.... The situation was assuming a nightmare quality. This man, this Brent Sanders, clearly had some deep and devious reason for fearing she had lied. Donna couldn't begin to imagine what it was. But she, equally, and for good reasons of her own, didn't want anyone to know where she was. She looked at him, and the dismay she felt must have shown in her eyes, for she saw his face change, become almost grim, and for the second time she felt fear, only now it was more tangible. She was caught in a situation that was no longer simple and clear-cut.

She took a deep breath. 'I can't,' she said.

'Can't tell me who you are?'

'No.'

A muscle moved in his dark, bearded jaw. 'Your plane has identification,' he said softly. 'I'll check up on that.'

She looked at him. 'No—I——'

'It hasn't?'

'Yes. Not that—I——' She pushed the comb away, almost without being aware of what she was doing. 'I spoke the truth. I'm here only for—a holiday——'

'And there's something remarkably suspicious about you,' he cut in.

'No!' She stood up, too tense to remain seated. 'No. I'm——' she put her hand to her mouth. If he knew who she was—she shouldn't have landed. She should have spotted the boat and taken off again immediately. Agitated, she turned away to look out of the window. Her plane bobbed at rest, and the numbers on the wings were almost visible from here, but too angled to see clearly.

'What the hell gives?' he demanded angrily, and whirled her round to face him. His eyes had darkened, almost black, and his face was deadly serious.

'I've run away from—something—a situation—I don't want anyone to know—please believe me——'

He let her arm go abruptly. 'You expect me to believe *that*?' he demanded.

'Yes. *Yes*, I do! It's the truth!'

'Then tell me. Let me be the judge——'

'You wouldn't understand. A man wouldn't——'

His lip curled scornfully. 'You're on the run?'

'Nothing criminal——'

'From a man, then?'

She went very still. 'In a way.'

'That's not good enough. It either is or it isn't.'

'Then—yes.'

'Your husband? Lover?'

'I'm not married. Yes, there's a man—but he's not the only reason I'm here——'

'You're not even making sense,' he grated.

'I shouldn't have to, to *you*. I know. I understand why I'm here. But you wouldn't——'

'Understand? You've already said that.' He seemed to be fast losing what little patience he appeared to possess. He was large and frightening to Donna, because nothing like this had ever happened to her before. Nothing quite like this. She never had to give reasons, explain herself to anyone. Yet here, now, she felt as if she were fighting for her sanity. And Brent Sanders had made it clear that she had to tell him everything. But how could she when she couldn't even put it into words? Nonie had understood, but then she had always been so perceptive that half the time words weren't needed. She already knew, she sensed, and her intuition was strong. But if she didn't tell him the truth, he wasn't going to let her go anyway, and Donna didn't doubt his power or ability to do exactly as he wished. For he too had a secret, it seemed, and believed she was here to spy on him, and would take a lot of convincing otherwise. If he was not a criminal, what could his secret be? She couldn't even attempt to guess. She was too tired—and beginning to feel confused after the strong beer on an empty stomach.

She sat down again, wearily, exhausted. 'My first name is Donna,' she said. 'I'd rather you didn't know my surname—please bear with me, and I'll explain my situation.'

He watched her, but said nothing, then he fetched two more cans of beer from the refrigerator, put them on the table, and sat down. Donna looked at him. He pointed towards one tin, a question in his eyes, and she nodded. 'Yes, please,' she said. She watched him fill her glass. His hands were large and very strong-looking, yet he held the glass with care. He could crush it if he were not careful. He could crush her if he chose, and it would be no effort for him, and there was no way she could fight him, even with an armoury of weapons to defend herself. He had an aura of such power and strength and dominance about him that she doubted he would believe her. Even though his reasons for being here were obviously secret, he hadn't run away from anything. It made him seem almost sinister, for why then should he not want her to leave, and be determined to prevent her? Who was he? She wondered if she would ever know. One thing was sure: there was no way she could make him tell her anything if he chose not to.

She sipped at the sharp tingly beer, and felt slightly better. And now she had to take the plunge.

'I lead a life that may sound strange to you,' she began. 'I come from a family who are—different from most. My father, my uncles, my grandfather—all winners. I've been brought up to regard winning as very important. I've got two sisters, and they're the same. All our lives we've had the best of everything, and we accepted it as our due—because we knew no different. I've travelled all over the world, I learnt to fly when I was eighteen, and I've motor-raced, and skied, and competed in just about everything, and enjoyed every moment of it.' She paused to sip her beer, while Brent Sanders said nothing, merely watched her. He sat very still, and his eyes were hard and dark and seemed to look right inside her, and she wasn't sure if she was frightened of him or not.

'I never questioned my life-style. I enjoyed it, as did my sisters. We had everything, you see. And then my father introduced me to the man he had decided would make me an ideal husband.' She felt her mouth tighten slightly. 'I didn't particularly like this man— but he——' she hesitated. This was going to be difficult. 'He—fell for me rather hard. He's connected in business with our family, he's thirty, and good-looking—and he's a winner too, just like I've always been, and if I'd have fallen for him it would have been all right. But I didn't. And the more I told him I wasn't interested the more obsessed he became about me. My father was getting angry too, and it made me realise a lot about the life I'd never before questioned. My two sisters are married—again to men that Daddy had "hinted" might be ideal. But they're not particularly happy. They have affairs, and so do their husbands—and I suddenly realised that I couldn't go on living this kind of shallow existence——' She stopped and gripped her glass tightly, trying to regain her self-possession.

Then Brent Sanders spoke. He had been listening, but now he spoke.

'I know who you are,' he said.

CHAPTER TWO

DONNA stared at him, wide-eyed, disbelieving. How could he know?

'How?' she asked.

'The Webster family is famous,' he remarked dryly. 'Is that why you didn't want to tell me your surname?'

She had gone icily cold, yet her skin was damp with perspiration. 'How did you guess?' she asked, dully, still numb with shock.

'Your christian name is unusual. It rang a bell—I'd read something about you recently in a paper. Some party in Greece attended by royalty—and you had your photo in the gossip columns the following day. It wasn't a good likeness——' Donna remembered the photograph well. No, it hadn't been a good likeness, fortunately. She was, in the photo, just emerging from the swimming pool with very little on, and she had been drunk. She had been furious at the time—but since then, in a way, it had helped to crystallise her urge to get away from that life. For she had seen it again recently, and had felt such revulsion at everything——

'But I remembered it.' Brent Sanders gazed at her steadily. 'I can well imagine you wanting to escape.'

'You don't know the half of it,' she said bitterly.

'I don't think I want to. The man who's obsessed by you—was he the one with you at the party? Steven something?'

'Steven Foxe-Lennard.' She stared into her glass as

she heard Brent open his own can of beer. 'Yes, he was.'

'And now you've run away. Why?' he asked bluntly. 'Were you afraid of him?'

'In a way—yes.' She raised her eyes to him. 'Does that surprise you?'

'A little. Having met you—yes, it does. I'd have thought you capable of telling him to go to hell.'

She smiled faintly. 'I told you you wouldn't understand. I did just that. I finished with him, and I told Daddy I had. Only Steven never takes no for an answer, and he's besotted with me for some reason. He's *obsessed*.'

She heard his indrawn breath. 'He's what?' he asked.

'I think you heard. Yes, Mr Sanders, I mean every word. He told me that he didn't accept that, that *I* was crazy, that I would come to my senses, and that he was going to marry me. Then came a relentless bombardment, of flowers, letters, phone calls—I'd go to a restaurant for a meal with friends, and he'd be there. He had me followed. I told my father and he laughed it off, said I was exaggerating, said I ought to be flattered at the attention—that I'd always been spoiled and it was time I grew up. Money is very important to my father, and my marriage to Steven would mean an interesting—and profitable—merger. Daddy thought I was playing hard to get, while I, meanwhile, was beginning to realise the shallowness and hypocrisy of just about everyone I'd always trusted. I had to get away, to think clearly, so I travelled to my godmother who lives in Barbados—I managed to give Steven the slip, but I knew it wouldn't be for long. Then I hired a seaplane and flew here.'

'And only your godmother knows where you are?'

'Yes.' She traced a pattern on the table with a drop of spilled liquid. 'Now do you believe me?'

'Yes. It's too bizarre to have been made up.'

'Thanks.' Her tone was dry. 'It doesn't explain why you're so suspicious of strangers, does it?'

'No. But then it wasn't intended to.'

'Aren't you going to tell me?'

Brent shook his head. 'And are you going to let me go?' she asked.

'No.'

The answer, the one short word, was a shock. Her head jerked back. 'What?'

'Stay. You'll be—safer here.' She didn't like the way he hesitated before the last words, and her eyes narrowed, became wary.

'Safer? From what?'

'He might have followed you. You've no guarantee——'

'And I'd be safer with you?'

He smiled thinly. 'You'll be a hell of a sight safer than if you were all alone and he arrived—if he's as obsessed as you say.'

'He is,' she answered shortly. This wasn't the reason he wanted her to stay, it was a smokescreen.

'And are you lovers?'

Her mouth tightened. 'Is that any business of yours?'

'Not particularly, but I'm curious. Are you?'

She didn't know why she was answering him. 'No, we're not,' she replied. 'Satisfied?'

He shrugged. 'In your world, I wouldn't have thought it mattered to you, a question like that.'

'You don't know what my world is like,' she said quietly.

'I've heard enough from you to know it wouldn't appeal to me.'

'Then perhaps you understand why I had to get away—to be alone.'

'Yes. Sorry to disappoint you.'

'I don't believe you want me to stay solely out of concern,' she added.

'Don't you?'

'No. But you're not going to tell me the real reason, are you?'

'No, I'm not. I'll be here a week or so more. So will you. When we leave, we'll go our separate ways. Just accept that.'

'You don't want anyone to know you're here.' It was a statement, not a question.

'I should have thought I'd made that obvious.'

'Yet you're not a criminal.'

'No, I'm not.' He looked at the clock on the wall of the galley. 'It'll be getting dark soon. Hadn't you better get your things unloaded?'

'They're on the beach. I came looking for you immediately I'd landed.'

'And where are you planning to sleep?'

'Nonie told me there's an old bungalow farther along.'

He shook his head gently, and she frowned. 'What? Isn't there?'

'Oh, there's a building—of sorts—but it's rotten, quite unsafe. Think again.'

'I can sleep on the plane,' Donna insisted.

'You can sleep aboard here. There's plenty of room.'

'No, thanks,' she answered promptly.

'As you wish.' He stood up, as if it were a matter

of complete indifference to him. 'Do you want any help?'

'I'll manage. Thanks for the beer, it was just what I needed.'

'You're welcome.' His tone was dry.

'I'd like to see the bungalow. Will you show me?'

'Of course.'

He led the way out, and down the side, and they waded through warm shallow water ashore. Brent looked at the plane, then at her possessions on the beach, but said nothing.

Five minutes' walk along the sand brought them to the derelict bungalow, and as she saw it, Donna's heart sank. She thought he might have exaggerated its disrepair, simply to have her within sight of him, but one glance was enough to tell her it wasn't fit to enter, let alone live in. The plane would be cramped, and she would have to build a fire on the beach if she wanted to cook food, and wash in the sea, and she wished that she hadn't been so hasty in refusing his offer.

'You were right, it's useless,' she said, as he turned and began to walk back towards the bay where he was moored.

'Yes. How will you manage?'

'I'll manage. I always have done.' She gave a shrug to show that she was perfectly capable of roughing it which clearly didn't fool him for a moment, for he laughed.

'It'll be interesting to see. Are you used to camping out?'

She stopped walking and turned to face him. 'You seem to find this quite funny,' she snapped. 'I'm glad something amuses you!'

'Temper,' he chided. 'Don't try that with me.

You're not with your usual crowd now, remember? I'm the one with the boat. If you change your mind you might be better advised to watch that sharp tongue of yours——'

'I won't,' she retorted. 'I can look after myself perfectly well without your help.' She didn't like him any more than she had done when she arrived, and his story of Steven following her was a feeble one to say the least—and she had decided that she wasn't going to stay here with him. At first light in the morning she would go, before he awoke. She would find a suitable island nearby—there was a detailed large scale map in the plane that would help—and go there. She did, after all, want to be alone, and she wasn't having anyone dictating to her, least of all him.

Thus decided, she became more relaxed. She even managed to smile at him. He really was a tough-looking customer. She would like to see his face in the morning when he discovered her gone.

'I'm sorry,' she said. 'Look, let me make a meal for us both, with my food, and eat it on your boat. Will that make amends?'

'It sounds remarkably civilised to me,' he agreed. 'And while you're cooking it, would you like me to load your stuff back on the plane? It's not safe to leave out all the time, there are creepy-crawlies that come out at night.'

That decided her; she would definitely not sleep on the beach. She shuddered. 'Please!'

An hour later it was pitch black outside, but inside the galley a warm light glowed, and Donna and Brent ate steak and salad and drank his wine, and all was well— on the surface. He seemed more relaxed, had had a shave and put a shirt on, and was a far less fearsome character than the one she had seen asleep on the boat. She still knew absolutely nothing about him. The other difference was that she no longer wanted to. She conceded, as she took away the plates at the end of the meal, that some women might even find him attractive. He had the kind of face that friends of hers would find interesting—tough, yes, but with that kind of toughness that tells of character within. Strong features, tanned and hard, and a chin that was decidedly stubborn, with a cleft in it. And when she had cooked the steak and prepared the salad, he had commented on it, had thanked her—had been almost gentlemanlike in behaviour, a strong contrast to his previous manner.

Now the meal was over, and it was time to leave. She would not see him again, but he didn't know that. She yawned prettily, and apologised.

'You'll have to excuse me, I'm very tired,' she said.

'Of course. The invitation still stands. There's a cabin ready for visitors.'

'I'm tempted—but no, thanks. I prefer to be alone.' And I can leave with less fuss in the morning, she added to herself.

'Of course. I'll see you ashore. I've got a torch here somewhere. All your stuff is on the plane.' He opened a drawer and brought out a large rubber-covered torch. 'Ready?'

'Yes.' She followed him over the side and he held out his hand to help her. They waded ashore, then along, and out towards the plane. His torch beam lit up the door and she climbed up and opened it.

'Goodnight, Brent,' she said.

'Goodnight.' Donna closed the door and saw the

torch beam moving away. She looked at her watch, made a mental note to wake at six, and prepared her sleeping bag. Five minutes later she was asleep.

When she awoke, after a restless uncomfortable night, it was barely dawn. All was quiet and still everywhere, and she began to work, by the dim light of her own torch, checking the map first, washing in the minuscule lavatory at the rear of the plane, and dressing rapidly. It was barely six. Soon the sun would be up, and it would be too late, for Brent woke early, a fact she had established over their dinner. Then all was ready. An unnamed island lay eleven miles north-west of Paradise Island, and there was, according to the map, fresh water on it. She was going there to stay.

She checked the controls, fastened her seat-belt, and said a little prayer for a quick safe getaway, switched on and waited for the engine to warm up. There was a whirr, a hollow, strange sound, then silence. Heart beating rapidly, she tried again, with the same result. The engines were dead. Donna unfastened her seat-belt, opened the door and, moving cautiously, edged her way along towards the engines. There must be a loose connection somewhere——

'Good morning,' said a cheerful, wide-awake voice. 'Having trouble?' She looked round, clutching a spar, startled, to see Brent sitting on the beach watching her. Then—*then* she knew.

Furious, she swung down, waded ashore, and stalked over to him. He rose gracefully to his feet as she reached him. 'What have you done?' she demanded furiously, eyes sparking fire.

'Done?' he asked, tone innocent. 'What do you mean?'

'Damn you—damn you!' She swung her arm round and gave him a stunning slap on his face, and he caught her hand and held it tightly, and even in that dull, pre-dawn light, she saw the whiteness of temper on his features.

Then, so suddenly that it caught her breath in her throat, he swung her up into his arms and carried her, kicking, struggling and screaming, towards his boat. He hefted her on to the deck as if she were a sack of potatoes and leapt over the rail beside her. 'Get down below,' he commanded. 'Now—before I lose my temper.'

'Go to hell!' She whirled away, but he caught and held her, then picked her up under one arm and walked down into the galley with her. There he released her, slammed shut the door, and leaned against it.

'So,' he said. 'You were leaving without saying goodbye?'

'Yes, I damned well was! What did you do to the plane?'

'Not a lot. I removed a small but rather vital part from the engine while you were cooking that delightful meal last night. I did tell you you were staying.' He looked reproachfully at her. 'And you said you would.' His manner, the way he said the words, only served to infuriate her more—as he must have known, because a spark of amusement lit his eyes.

'I changed my mind,' she said, seething, but still with enough control to know that losing her temper wouldn't help her at all. 'I'm a free woman, not your prisoner, as you seem to think. Please replace the part you removed.'

'No.'

She took a deep breath. 'You can't do this! I—I can have you up for kidnapping.'

'Probably, when we leave. Not here, though. No police——'

'For God's sake stop being facetious! You're hateful——'

'You're childish. There's room for us both here, and you'll have no trouble from Steven if he does come after you——'

'He won't.'

'You can't guarantee it, it's essential that you stay. No one must know I'm here. How can I be sure you won't tell? You've already proved your ability for deception by trying to sneak off——'

'I wish I'd never come!' she grated.

'So do I. But you have—which fact is hardly *my* fault. All I'm ensuring is that my privacy is kept intact. I'm not going to torture you, harass you, or annoy you. You can wander about as you please, do what you will, swim, sunbathe, have a holiday, in fact. You can also sleep in a comfortable bed and have proper showers, which you damn well wouldn't have been able to do if you were alone. So why are you fighting me so hard?'

'Because, Mr Clever Know-it-all-Sanders, I object strongly to being *made* to do anything. And whether you admit it or not, you're acting in a high-handed manner, telling me I *mustn't* leave. That's why I'm fighting, and will continue to fight, so don't think I'm going to agree meekly with you, because I'm not, and I never will.'

'Then we'll be here all that much longer. The choice is yours. Keep out of my hair, I'll keep out of yours, and I'll be finished sooner.'

'Finished at what?' she demanded.

'At what I'm doing.'

'Which is?'

Brent tapped his nose. 'Ah! There's the question.'

Trembling, Donna went over to him. Before she could even attempt to put her fury into action, he had caught and was holding both her hands. 'Going to hit me again? I wouldn't if I were you. I'm getting a bit fed up of being socked in the face without being able to retaliate.'

'I've hit you *once*——' she began, seething.

'And that was quite enough. I've got a temper to match yours, and I might just hit back, and you wouldn't like that, I promise you.'

'You wouldn't dare!' she glared at him.

'Wouldn't I? Try me.' He released her hands and remained where he was, and just for a moment, she was tempted. Just for a moment. The expression on his face was a strange one. The thought of being struck by him made her feel almost ill. Would he? There was one way to find out—but she dared not.

'You—*beast*!' she spat.

'At least you've controlled your hands—that's a start. You might yet learn a few manners while you're here.' The corner of his mouth twitched. 'And I may teach you.'

'Not you. There's nothing you can teach me,' she seethed.

'Isn't there? You'll see.' Then he put his hand up and patted her cheek. It was the slightest tap, but it seemed a calculated gesture—an insult, and Donna stepped back as though he had in fact struck her, and he laughed. A deep amused, mocking laugh. That did it. Nerves frayed from the shock discovery of finding he had removed part of her engine so that she couldn't get away, and suddenly incensed beyond all reason, and forgetting his threat, she lashed out at him—and the next moment he grabbed her, caught and held her, pulled her towards him, and kissed her violently. She reeled from the shock as he released her, and staggered back, eyes welling with tears at the savagery and suddenness of the kiss. Panting, she stared at him, wordless, and he glared back at her. 'Perhaps that's a better way than hitting you,' he said, with contempt, then he wiped his mouth with the back of his hand. His eyes were like flint. 'Had enough?' he taunted. 'Or shall I do it again?'

Donna looked round for something to throw at him, but there was nothing. She marched forward to the door and opened it. He slammed it shut before she could go out, and said: 'You leave here when I say so, you little wildcat.'

'I'm not staying in here with *you*!' she breathed. 'Open that door!'

'When you learn some manners,' he answered, more calm than she, apparently. 'And as you *are* staying, I suggest you learn some fast. We might as well get on together——'

'Get on with *you*? I'd rather die——'

'Don't be childish. My God, no wonder you wanted to escape—the only thing you don't seem to realise is they were probably delighted to see you go.' His tone was hard, inexorable, and she had no choice but to listen. Wide-eyed, face white, she remained standing where she was as the shocking words came at her. Then they hit her. He meant them. It was as if she saw her life unfolding before her in a never-ending film that went back, and back ... relentless, nothing hidden, the life that had led her to this situation, and this man here in this place.

Donna sat down. Silently Brent went and opened a cupboard and brought out a glass and a bottle. He poured in a measure and handed it to her. 'Drink that,' he said. 'It'll do you good.' It was rum, hot and sweet and strong. Donna obediently drank, then he sat opposite her at the table. 'I spoke the truth before,' he said. 'I said it brutally because it was the only way you would listen. And now I'm going to tell you why I'm here, and why you must stay.'

Donna, still shocked, looked at him silently. It didn't seem to matter; nothing did any more. She ached inside with a deep pain which refused to go away. It hurt so much that she laid her hand across her stomach.

'I'm here looking for treasure.' The words didn't register. She sat there, and pressed her hand to her body as if to make the ache go away. 'Two hundred years ago, a boat went down in the Caribbean Sea— but no one knew exactly where. It was carrying gold bullion from Spain to Cuba. After various sorts of detective work with which I will not bore you, I've located the ship—or its remains. It's in ten fathoms of water a mere hundred yards from here. For obvious reasons I don't want anyone else to know its whereabouts yet. Not until I've done all I can. There's a reward for the recovery of the gold, and I'm intending to claim it.'

'You're mad.' The words came out quietly, almost of their own volition. 'Treasure? It sounds like a boys' adventure story!'

'So it does. Except that it happens to be true.' Brent walked away from her and opened another cupboard. From it he took several photographs which he laid on the table. 'Look at those.'

Donna did so. They were underwater photographs—blurred, yet the hulk of a ship was visible, dark and forbidding, and in another, a nearer view, of a gaping hole in the side. Fish swam near the camera, frozen in a second of time. 'You took these?'

'Yes. It's the *Maria Grande* all right.' He took the photographs back.

'And you're working alone?'

'I usually do.'

'Usually? You've—done this before?'

'Yes.'

'Successfully?'

'Yes.'

'Who *are* you?' she demanded.

'I've told you my name—Brent Sanders. What more do you want to know?'

'Is this how you make your living?' she asked.

'No. It's a hobby.'

Donna looked up then, in scornful disbelief—and was halted by his expression. He smiled. 'You should learn to hide your contempt better. Not everyone outside your charmed circle is a peasant, Donna.'

She felt herself flush at the expression she saw in his eyes. He was too shrewd by far. He nodded as he saw her face. 'I see you understand.'

'I didn't mean——'

'Oh, but you did, only too clearly. You may be sick of your world, but you still possess the arrogant assumption of superiority of your kind.' He took the snaps and put them away and closed the cupboard. 'I could tell you more, but I won't. I feel no need to impress you. You know enough for now. Let's eat breakfast. I take it you didn't eat before your abortive

attempt at leaving?' She shook her head. 'Then we'll
have some food.'

'Are you diving today?' she asked in a quieter voice.
He had shaken her badly.

'Later, yes. Why?'

'Can I help?' She spoke on sudden inexplicable
impulse.

'I go down pretty deep,' he answered in dismissive
tones.

'I've done it before.'

'And you want to help me?'

'If you'll have me.'

'I don't want an hysterical woman on my hands.
The rules underwater will be obeyed—and I'm in
charge of the operation—we'll get that clear before we
begin.'

She nodded. 'I understand.'

'How deep have you been—and where—and when?'
He was slicing cheese thinly as he spoke, fetching out
jars from the refrigerator and putting the kettle on to
boil. He didn't seem to want help, and Donna
hesitated to offer.

'Two years ago I went diving off the coast of Crete
for some ancient artefacts sunk centuries before. We
went quite far down, I can't remember exactly, but we
had oxygen, and it took us nearly an hour to come up
again. There were four of us——'

'Jeremy Carrington in charge?'

She looked up, startled. 'Yes! You know him?'

'Slightly. I guessed it was him—I'd heard about
that trip. What got you on to it?'

'It seemed an amusing thing to do. I'd flown out to
stay with some friends who have a villa there, and met
him at a party. He was so full of enthusiasm that he

infected me with it, and the next thing I knew there I was walking about on the sea bed with a huge torch and fighting off octopus.' Donna smiled at the memory; she had enjoyed that unexpected adventure on an otherwise uneventful holiday.

'Okay, you'll do. I have two sets of diving equipment with me, for practical reasons. I've been near the wreck—yesterday as a matter of fact, which is why you caught me asleep. It's a slow, tiring process, coming up again. You will obey precisely my timing on that.'

'I know. I wouldn't dream of doing anything foolish.'

He looked at her. 'I believe, in that, you wouldn't. Eat now, Donna. We'll go down in two hours. Coffee?'

'Yes, please.'

'And now you're staying, and we'll be working together, you'd better move in here,' he added.

'Very well.' She buttered a piece of crispbread and spread the sweet apricot preserve on it.

'You've changed,' he remarked. 'You're very subdued. Why?'

She looked up at him. 'There's not much point in being otherwise, is there?'

'No. But I don't expect instant miracles.'

'I don't think there are any such things.' She gave a wry smile. 'You gave me some home truths before, and I haven't forgotten them.'

'I see. I may have been brutal. I wouldn't have hit you back, you know. Although I might have been tempted—I wouldn't have done it. Is that why you're so subdued?'

She shook her head. That was what he thought. He didn't know the truth then of his words, and how deeply they had gone home. And perhaps it was better this way. She suddenly realised, belatedly, something she should have known from the first moment she saw him. This man wasn't like any other she had ever encountered in her brief life. This man was force, and power, and a rapier-sharp mind and tongue. He was very probably afraid of nothing, and he had come here to be alone, not because he was running away, like her, but because he had something to do and was going to do it. Donna didn't doubt that he would succeed. She looked up at him, treacherous tears filling her eyes and brimming over.

'No, that's not why,' she said. 'I'd have deserved it anyway—I shouldn't have struck you. I apologise.'

'Violence has no part in my world,' he said softly. 'It's ugly. I abhor fighting. I didn't, at one time. I had a temper to match yours—still have, but now I keep it under control. That's something that life has taught me, among other things. There's too much of it in the world. That's why I prefer to work, and walk alone. You too will learn one day. Perhaps you already are, by breaking away from your life-style.'

'Running away, you mean,' she said.

'You had no choice, it seems to me. If that man Steven was so obsessed, you had to leave. When you go back, you'll know how to cope with people like him.'

'Will I? How?'

'I will have taught you,' he answered, and it sent a shiver up her spine. She believed him. She believed he could. She didn't know how, but it seemed that, with Brent Sanders, anything was possible. Anything.

CHAPTER THREE

Once they had eaten, and Donna had cleared away and washed the breakfast things, Brent vanished. He returned shortly afterwards and said: 'Come up on the beach. We'll have a crash course in sea diving.' Obediently Donna put down the magazine she had found and followed him overboard. In the shelter of the tall palms he had laid out the wet-suits, oxygen bottles, and cutting tools and a torch. 'Okay,' he told her. 'We'll get your stuff from the plane, you can change into a swimsuit—if you have one—and then get the wet-suit on. We may have to do some adjusting all round. I'm larger than you.'

How true, she thought, but merely nodded. They waded through warm water to the plane, and once aboard Brent looked round with interest at the compact cabin. 'Did you *sleep*?' he enquired.

'Not very well. I was thinking about escape, I suppose.'

'And now you're not?'

She regarded him levelly. 'Not at the moment.'

His mouth quirked. 'I'm not sure what that means. Depending on how I behave myself?'

'Something like that,' she agreed.

He nodded. 'I don't fancy you,' he said bluntly. 'And I only make love to women I fancy——'

'You have a remarkably clear way of expressing yourself,' she cut in tartly.

'Would you prefer it if I did?' He cocked an eyebrow, amused.

'I don't give a damn either way.' Donna gave a little smile. 'I don't fancy you either.'

'That's hardly surprising. I should think you're a bit off the male sex at the moment, which means our relationship won't be complicated by any undercurrents. Good—I work better with no distractions.' He picked up her box of food. 'Put your case on top, I can manage both.'

Donna did so. She was irritated by him, but not sure why. Perversely, she knew, because she really didn't like him, or his cavalier manner—but his blunt words had once again shaken her. He had the ability to do that with great ease, she decided, as she followed him with her rolled-up sleeping bag and toilet articles.

He showed her to the cabin next to his and told her he would put her food away while she changed. Donna closed the door and stripped off, then put on her sleek black one-piece swimsuit. She looked at herself in the wardrobe mirror. It was a reassuring sight for her flagging ego. Tall and slim, yet with full feminine curves, she was attractive, and knew it. She had always known it. All the Webster girls were beauties. She smoothed her dark auburn hair back, and pulled a face at her reflection. Round face, good high cheekbones faintly defined, large dark-lashed green eyes, a classical straight nose and soft full mouth stared back at her impudently. She normally used make-up, but here it didn't matter. And yet on an impulse, remembering Brent's words, she took out her lipstick and smoothed some on. It was a pinky-beige shade, very fashionable, and it suited her. She was ready.

He was waiting for her on the beach, smoking a small cigar. Dressed in the shorts he had worn the previous day, he stood there unaware at first that she had emerged from her cabin, and for a few moments Donna looked at him unobserved. He made a striking picture, the big man standing there watching a small brightly coloured bird darting at flowers in a shrub. His legs were long and well muscled, his thighs as solid as any athlete's, and he was standing sideways; his waist and hips were lean, but his chest was broad. Shoulders heavy. He would pack quite a punch if he wanted to, was her sudden irrational thought—which was ridiculous, because he had told her he abhorred violence. His over-long shaggy black hair clearly hadn't been combed that morning, and the sun caught it, and it shone with a faint touch of gold. The hawklike profile was pensive. He turned suddenly, although Donna hadn't made a sound that she was aware of, and he looked at her, a brief all-encompassing glance that took in every detail of her appearance, and she climbed over the rail and jumped into the water and waded ashore, fully conscious of his scrutiny. The front of her slim-fitting suit was low and scooped, and for a brief moment his eyes remained on her cleavage—as if he couldn't help it. She hid her smile as she went over to him.

'Bird-watching?' she asked, voice innocent, smiling faintly. The bird darted away, startled by her voice, and her words were clearly meant for that, and nothing else, and he nodded.

'Living things have always interested me. Now, get the suit on, and we'll see if we need to make many adjustments.' Donna sat down to ease on the legs of the one-piece suit. The smell of rubber was strong, and she wrinkled her nose. She stood, pulled on the top, and fastened up the thick zip, then stood there. She felt like a balloon. The legs were far too long, it was loose round her body and shoulders, and the sleeves, which should have been as tight-fitting as the legs, were equally baggy. She was roasting within seconds. She looked down at herself in dismay.

'Mmm,' Brent nodded, and it was hard to tell if he was stifling laughter. 'We have slight problems, I think.' It seemed to be quite an understatement.

'Some,' she agreed. 'What do we do?'

'Apart from putting you on an instant weight-gaining diet, which isn't very practical, I can only suggest we find a way of adjusting arm and leg ends,' he said, and knelt. She watched him, as with impersonal fingers he began to ease the baggily fitting legs down, then roll up the ends round her ankles. He looked up at her. 'It needs to be watertight on your limbs,' he said, 'as you know. I'll have to tape you up. Stay there, don't move.' He went to the boat, climbed aboard, and vanished. Donna, perspiring freely now, waited patiently. He knew what he was doing, no doubt about that. She was going to be too busy to have time to think about her life, or Steven, she was already beginning to realise that—and it was no bad thing. This man, Brent Sanders, was like a human bulldozer. She had a sudden vision of being taped up, trussed like a chicken from top to toe, and she smiled. He reappeared, came over and waded to her, holding a large roll of black tape.

'Hold it a moment,' she said. 'This is a practice, right?'

He nodded. 'Well,' she went on, 'hadn't we better leave the trussing up until we're actually ready to go under? It will save wasting tape.'

'Quite right. Are you boiling?'

'Yes.'

'Okay, strip off. I'll show you round the island until our breakfast's digested, and in future we'll skip food, get an early morning start before the sun gets too hot and eat after. Agreed?'

Donna was peeling off the now hot wet-suit as he spoke, and dropped it thankfully. 'Phew! That's better.' Her face was pink, she knew that. I'm crazy, she thought. I've actually volunteered for this madness. She smoothed a hand across her forehead.

'We'll go and collect our day's supply of water,' Brent told her, and pointed to several large plastic containers at the base of a tall tree. They carried three each, and although cumbersome, they were light. He led the way into the trees, and although it was slightly cooler in the shade, it was still hot. Donna followed, and they went gently upwards through sandy soil, with branches and leaves catching at her arms and legs, and insects buzzing around angrily. She wondered how well she would have fared alone. She had every confidence in her own ability to look after herself, and had always been independent, but there was something rather pleasant in having everything taken charge of by this big, tough, unusual man who definitely didn't fancy her—she wondered why she should think of that, and shrugged off the thought. Stupid, she told herself.

'Nearly there,' he said, without looking round. 'Scared of creepy-crawlies?'

'Not particularly,' she answered. 'Why?'

'There are a lot of spiders hereabouts. Not deadly— I don't think so anyway—but rather large ones with hairy legs.' Like you, she thought, and couldn't stifle the sudden laughter that erupted, and when he turned round to look at her, she said:

'Just a thought I had.' There was absolutely no point in telling him. He would be very good with the perfect squelch. There was a nice truce in existence. She wasn't going to do anything to spoil it. Then they emerged from the trees and ahead was an open space with the crystal waterfall emerging from high rocks to tumble into a wide oval rock-surrounded pool.

'Oh!' The exclamation was involuntary. 'It's beautiful!'

'So it is.' Brent flung down the containers. 'Come on in, it's only a few feet deep.' He stepped over the protecting rock wall and into the water, and Donna followed. The water was sparkling in the sunlight, and she sat down and splashed herself freely. Brent did the same, running his fingers through his soaking hair. 'I have a bath here most evenings,' he told her. 'It's better than sea-water. You can do the same.' Then he looked at her in mock severity. 'I mean, of course, at separate times.'

'Of course.' She lifted one eyebrow in pretended shock. She cupped her hands and splashed the water on her face and shoulders, then she lay back so that her long thick hair was taken, and floated round her face and neck. 'Mmm, bliss,' she murmured. She sat up suddenly, to see that he was looking at her, and he wasn't smiling. He looked away, towards the waterfall.

'We'd better fill up and go,' he said, and stood up. Donna felt a sudden pang of dismay. She wondered if she had done anything to displease him. For a moment there had been something like anger on his face, and in his eyes, before he had turned away from her. She scrambled to her feet, not understanding why she should suddenly feel anxious not to provoke his disapproval.

'Yes. I'll pass you the containers,' she said, and scrambled out of the pool. This was ridiculous. She felt absurdly like a child who had just been scolded by a teacher, and was now anxious to please.

She handed him an empty container and watched him fill it from the gushing waterfall from the rocks, took it full from him and handed him the second, which he filled as she screwed on the lid.

When they were all full his brief and disturbing moment of apparent anger had gone. 'I'll carry four,' he said, 'if you can manage two. They're heavy,' he added unnecessarily as she picked two up. They were. He held one under each arm and one in each hand and didn't seem to find them at all heavy. 'Ready?' he asked.

'Yes.'

He turned and walked away without another word, and the journey back to the boat was accomplished in silence. When the water was stowed away aboard, he said: 'I'll show you round, although it's all pretty much the same.'

'Then let's leave it for now, shall we?' Donna looked at the waiting equipment. 'It's nearly time to dive, isn't it?'

'As you wish.' He looked at his watch. 'Nearly nine. We'll dive until we're tired.'

She put on the suit, and then came the moment she half dreaded, the moment when he was going, of necessity, to touch her. She didn't want the personal contact; she didn't know exactly why.

Brent had a knife, and he knelt at her feet and began operations. She stood there very still as he tightened the endings of the suit and taped them firmly. 'Tell me if it feels too tight,' he said, as he finished her left ankle.

'No, it's fine,' she answered, and he did the same with her right leg. Then he stood up. She could feel the perspiration trickling down her inside the suit, although in several minutes, when they were diving, she would be glad of the insulation and would need it.

She held up her right arm and he concentrated on his task. He was standing close to her, again because of necessity, but it was all very impersonal and he wasn't even looking at her, only her sleeve, and hand, as he worked, but she was looking at him, and it was disturbing to her. She was so close that she could see a faint hairline scar on his forehead going into his hair, the thick hair that sprang darkly from his head. She could see his tanned skin, the faint lines at the corners of his eyes, as if he laughed a lot or was used to looking long distances. His lashes were thick, not long, but thick, and the grey eyes had darker, almost black flecks in them. She felt his breath on her face, and there was the faintest lingering smell of cigars mingling with minty toothpaste. She suddenly jerked her arm away, not knowing why, and he asked:

'Did I hurt you?'

'No.' She didn't understand her involuntary movement, except perhaps that she had wanted to free herself of his nearness, and the deed had followed on the wish.

'Nervous?' Faint mockery tinged his voice.

'Of course not.' She gave him back her hand, and watched his fingers at work because she didn't want to see his face any more. He wound the tape tightly so that no water could get in, or air escape. Donna's lips tingled at the sudden unexpected memory of his kiss, and she felt her face go warmer than before, and took a deep, dismayed breath. This was utterly ridiculous!

Her heart was beating so hard and fast that she wondered he didn't remark on it, but he didn't. Men didn't have this effect on her. Not this. She enjoyed flirting, romancing, kissing, but on a superficial level. No man had ever roused the deeper wanting within her, and she had never committed herself to one. Therefore this feeling, so disturbing, was alien and very puzzling to her, and she became uneasy.

It was a relief to be finished at last, and making their way out by a small dinghy to the spot over the wreck. 'All right?' asked Brent, and she nodded. With skin-tight rubber cap on he looked faintly sinister, but then, thought Donna, I bet I don't look particularly glamorous either. He went backwards over the side, with a splash that rocked the boat, and after a momentary hesitation she followed suit.

She wore a weighted belt, and her torch was clipped on to it, and as she swam strongly down, nose and mouthpiece firmly in place, she was in another world, a world of soft wavering shadows and greenness, gradually deepening, becoming blurred and hazy. Fish swam past, some indifferent, others flipping away rapidly in alarm, and Brent waited for her a few yards beneath her until she reached him. They were nearly at bottom now, and he took her hand as they kicked and drifted downwards, until their feet touched. She could see almost nothing. What light that reached was so faint as to be almost useless, like daylight obscured by thick pea-souper fog. A beam of yellow light suddenly pierced the gloom, and Donna experienced a strange thrill as she saw the dark bulk outlined ahead. Walking now, weightless, they went forward—then she saw the enormity of the task.

The ship was encrusted with barnacles and stony

fossil-like shapes, on every available inch of its surface. Thick weeds grew up from the sea-bed, giant seaweed twining and twisting in the current, and there seemed no possible way to get nearer. Holding Brent's hand, she inched forward until the high rough wall was dead ahead. Brent pulled gently towards the right, his torch beam casting a path, and she followed, along, along for what seemed like ever, but was probably several minutes. He flashed the beam upwards and she saw the raw gaping hole in that solid hulk. He pointed upwards, and they swam up, and then in.

This was frightening. Her impulse was to panic and flee, to escape, to go up and up to the surface—she fought it, and felt his grasp tighten on her hand as if he sensed her terror.

There were no sounds here. It was a deadly silent world with only the drumming inside her head and ears, and the pounding of her own heart, as though she could feel the blood coursing through her veins. The beam stabbed through the darkness and she saw another hole, this time regular in shape, clearly a hatchway. Weeds clung to the wooden surface, and a jellyfish floated past, near her face, and she flinched. Then—through, and walking along what had been walls, or ceiling, for the ship was well over on to one side, and Donna was disorientated with the weightlessness. Diving off Crete hadn't been like this. They hadn't gone so deep, or inside an enclosed space, it had been merely a case of digging the sea-bed.

She was frightened. She was more frightened than she had ever been before in her life, and she was resisting the fear with all the power she possessed. Brent was searching for something, his torch beam probing the limits of their prison, then he released her hand and swam away, while Donna, terrified, followed, and nearly cannoned into him when he stopped, crouching down.

He stood up and pressed the torch into her hands, and pointed it to a corner; she nodded that she understood, and held it, frightened lest it waver with her own tremors. She saw him unclip an axe from his belt, and just as suddenly as it had come, the fear left her. He wasn't afraid. He was intent on his task, which appeared to be hacking through a door which was jammed fast shut. Movement was slow, almost painfully so. She sensed the effort it was for him to force the axe in the wood, and as she saw it more clearly, became aware that he was taking up again something he had already started. Marks were already in the heavy solid wood. He was adding to them with each swing of the axe.

He stopped after a few minutes and rested, then began again. Donna wanted to help, but was aware that her own efforts would have been puny beside his. The fact that he had her holding the torch was clearly a help to him. She wondered how he had managed before. Perhaps wedged it somewhere.

While watching his steady efforts, she had time to think. To think about her life, and the way it had been, and the arrogance of her family and friends. He had been right there. What was it he had said? 'You still possess the arrogant assumption of superiority of your kind.' No one had ever said words like that to her before. No one had ever said a truth like that. She wouldn't have listened if anyone had, she would have laughed as at something ridiculous. But she hadn't been able to laugh at Brent when he said them. She had been made to listen. A brief flare of anger filled her. Who did he think *he* was? Someone superior? She watched him at work, a dark bulky outline in the confines of the small space, leaning forward now to wrench a giant portion of rotted wood from its base, and she knew she might not have been there, for all the notice he was taking of her. She had no importance in his life, save perhaps at the moment as torch-bearer. But if she hadn't volunteered, he would have managed. It was a sobering thought.

Brent Sanders had no need of status, security, friends who said the things you wanted them to say. He was a true individual, a loner—a searcher. His boat was aptly named. And Donna knew, following swiftly on the heels of her previous thoughts, that she wanted him to like her. It was a sobering realisation. Why should she? She didn't know, but it was a fact.

She felt herself shiver, suddenly cold, and he turned towards her, then came nearer to her and signalled for her to come forward with her torch. She did so instantly, crouching down as he indicated, so that he could see precisely what he was doing. She held the torch steadily, to see his axe making headway in his powerful hands; she saw the hole gradually grow larger, until he was able to squeeze through. She waited, not knowing if he wanted her to follow, the fear returning. He had vanished completely, and she might have been alone in a watery world of darkness and pressure, and a weighting down on her. The beam wavered. The oxygen bubbles rose as she breathed carefully and slowly, willing herself not to panic. She must not panic. She must *not*. Where was he?

As she wondered, he reappeared, and, taking the torch from her, handed her her own and switched it on. Then he made a clear gesture for her to stay where she was, walked away, and vanished into the hole. That then became the worst time, the not knowing, just waiting. She felt her teeth chatter, and gripped the mouthpiece more firmly. Dear Lord, where was he? What was he *doing*?

It seemed an age before she saw the light growing again, then he reappeared, and took her hand, and they began to go back out the way they had come in.

It was well past noon. They had eaten, then rested, Donna in her cabin, Brent in his. She had thought she would not sleep, but no sooner had her head touched the pillow than she had gone out like a light. Now, an hour or so later, she opened her eyes and looked round her, for a moment not sure where she was. Then she remembered, and sat up. She still wore her swimsuit, and her body felt salty. She stripped, had a shower, and changed into sun-top and shorts. She was tanned, a light golden shade, and the black shorts and white top emphasised the tan. Quietly Donna walked past Brent's cabin, seeing his reflection in the mirror as she passed. He slept soundly as he had been the previous day.

They had surfaced from their search that morning, and she had been made aware of his complete authority as they did so. His timing was precise; Donna had been impatient, feeling that he was being unnecessarily cautious, and he had, at one stage, taken her arm and jerked her angrily towards him. When at last, they reached the dinghy, he had pulled off his mask and said: 'I thought I told you to do as you were told?'

Donna, pulling off her tightly fitting cap, had looked at him. 'So you did,' she answered. 'But really, there's no need to wait *quite* so long at every stage—'

'There is if I say so,' he had answered, and started the outboard motor, effectively silencing any reply she might have been tempted to make. It had annoyed her, and lunch had been a silent affair. Now, standing in the galley as she waited for the kettle to boil, Donna thought about him. There had been a quiet arrogance when he had answered her. It had riled her at the time, and still rankled. She was, after all, a volunteer helper. Did he have to be so bossy? The answer was apparently yes.

There was movement, footsteps, then he appeared in the doorway. 'Making tea?' he enquired.

'No, coffee. Want one?' she answered shortly.

He sat down as if unaware of the slight atmosphere. 'That will do me nicely.' He rubbed his face. 'Did you sleep?'

'Yes.' She had her back to him, and reached into the cupboard for two cups.

'Are you sunbathing for the rest of the day?' he asked.

'For a while, yes. Why?'

'I just wondered. I have work to do.'

Donna wondered what it was, but wasn't going to ask. That was, after all, the arrangement. They each went their own way—apart from the search in the mornings. For three hours or so they would be together, after that they would each do what they wanted to do.

She made the coffee and passed him his. For a moment she hesitated, wondering whether to sit down and drink her coffee with him, or take it to her cabin, and he lifted one eyebrow as if he sensed her indecision. 'Sit down,' he said mildly. 'I want to talk to you.'

She sat down, feeling a twinge of resentment. 'Yes?' she said. 'What about?'

Brent regarded her very levelly over his cup, and again she had the uncomfortable sensation of being under close scrutiny—almost of having her mind read. He smiled slightly. 'About obedience,' he murmured. 'You got very stroppy this morning——'

'Because you took hours——'

He put his hand up. 'I hadn't finished,' he cut in. 'I did it for a reason. And you reacted just as I thought you would.'

Donna felt a flare of annoyance. 'Oh, I *see*,' she said with heavy irony. 'You were testing me?'

'Something like that,' he agreed calmly. 'I wanted to see if you could take orders—as you'd said you would. That was only our first dive together. It could have been our last.'

She jumped to her feet. 'You don't have to take me,' she flashed, temper rising. No one ever treated her like this! 'So why don't you go alone in future? I don't care.'

'Temper,' he murmured. 'It doesn't take much, does it? You've a very low flashpoint.'

'Go to hell,' she muttered, and picked up her coffee cup.

'And you don't like being told anything either. Shame. You did quite well on the dive too. I *had* great hopes.'

She had been about to walk out, but she stopped. A suddenly cold feeling swept over her. That was it. It was finished; his words made it clear. A shiver ran through her. It was as though he had just rejected her—and no one ever did that either. Brent looked up at her as she stood near the door, and she shrugged, to let him see that she didn't give a damn. 'That's life,' she said cynically. 'Some things work, some don't. I'll have more time for sunbathing——'

'And regaining your peace of mind,' he interrupted.

'Yes, indeed. What a pity you might never find it.'

'You have no right to say——' she began.

'I have every right to say what I want on *my* boat,' he reminded her. 'You have the right to walk away and not listen. You've never taken orders from anyone, have you? In your young life, it was what you wanted that counted. Only underwater there's a different discipline needed—it's not just a question of having fun, it's a question of life itself. We don't fool around with the sea. You should learn the difference between getting your own way in little things and behaving sensibly when it's important. I deliberately took extra time coming up to see what you would do. I got my answer. I don't want you with me again.' He finished his coffee and stood up, and walked over to the sink, while Donna watched him as though he had suddenly turned into a monster. There was a hard implacability about him that made her feel very vulnerable.

There was one question she had to ask. She wasn't going to beg or plead. She wondered if he thought she would. If so, he would be disappointed. She had never done that with anyone, and she wasn't going to start with him, but there was something she must do—and with dignity.

'I will, of course, leave your boat. That's what you expect, isn't it?'

'Don't be stupid, woman,' he snapped, and turned round. 'My God, when you get your dander up you really do it in style, don't you? I've got more room than I need, and as long as you keep out of my way you can stay. Do you honestly mean to say you'd be more comfortable in that cramped plane, cooking on the beach, than here?'

She could give him a scathing answer. She would tell him he could keep his boat, she would manage. But she knew that if she did, she would find her possessions removed faster than she could think about it. Pride struggled with practicality, and the latter won. She took a deep breath. 'I—I'd like to stay,' she said quietly at last, and with difficulty. Her innate pride didn't make the words easy to say.

Brent nodded, hiding amusement. 'You're learning,' he said dryly.

Donna bit her lip, stopping the quick retort that threatened to ruin everything. Then she walked over towards the sink, swallowed the last of her coffee, and rinsed both cups. Outwardly calm, inwardly seething—and in a strange way, feeling hurt, she wiped the cups with a tea-towel and put them away. 'I'll make a bargain with you,' said Brent, coming up behind her as he spoke. 'In return for your bed and board—and I've got lots of food, more than you, and certainly more than enough for us both—how do you feel about earning your keep?'

'How?' She turned towards him, lifting her chin, eyes calm as she looked at him. 'Housework? Cooking?'

'If you can cook—yes, and I think you're adequate at that. It will leave me free to do more diving—and other work. Don't worry, I don't expect you to put in an eight-hour day—just cook and tidy, nothing *you* couldn't manage.' There was an edge to his voice that she didn't like. Too subtle to remark on—yet there. Almost—patronising, almost humouring her.

'I can cook, yes,' she retorted coolly. 'And I'm quite sure I'm capable of making beds and washing up.' Her green eyes regarded him, and she watched his face, wondering why he should have the effect on her that he did. He was only a man, an aggressive, hard man who had made it plain that he regarded her as spoilt and childish, and she was ready to fight back after the humiliation she had just suffered. She had to remind herself that he was being sensible; it helped her to keep her face calm under his cool dark gaze.

'Then it's agreed? Good.' He nodded as though the matter, having been settled, could now be relegated somewhere else. He looked at his watch. 'Nearly four. Dinner at eight, I think. I'll leave the menu to you. I'm going to work up on deck.' He turned and went out.

Donna stood and watched him go. Thoughtfully she looked around the small, spotlessly clean galley. She had never done any cleaning before, although it had been fun to prepare the occasional meal for friends, after parties, when the staff had gone to bed. She had come here to forget everything, to recharge her batteries, to recover her strength and peace of mind. What was it Brent had said? 'What a pity you might never find it.' His words had been cruel, and they had hurt, and she wondered if it had been intentional that they should. She felt as if she were at a crossroads. She had come here expecting to be alone, and found him instead, and she wasn't free to go, because he didn't trust her, and he didn't want anyone to know he was there, so in a sense she was a prisoner.

She didn't like him, nor he her, that was clear. But

she didn't particularly like anyone else in the world
either at the moment, except Nonie, and she was far
away. She sat down very slowly at the table, feeling a
sudden great loneliness sweep over her. She put her
hands to her face, and a sob of despair escaped her.
The tears welled up, and she was powerless to stop
them, and her body was trembling with the sadness
that filled her. What was she going to do? How would
it all end? When Brent allowed her to leave—what
then? Perhaps there was no escape for her, ever. Just a
search for something, she knew not what; a seeking
and never finding. Brent was a man who knew where
he was going. He knew exactly—and as she had that
thought, she felt a hand touch her shoulder and started
in alarm. His voice came from behind her, almost
harsh:

'For God's sake, what's the matter *now*?' he asked.

CHAPTER FOUR

DONNA wiped hastily and furtively at her cheeks. She felt Brent's hand go from her shoulder. 'Nothing,' she said fiercely. 'I thought you'd gone——'

'So I see,' he answered. 'Is that why you were having a good blub? Feeling sorry for yourself? I could hardly avoid hearing all that——'

She jumped to her feet and faced him, 'I wasn't feeling sorry for myself,' she choked, 'I was—it was nothing—just a headache.'

'Is that how they affect you?' He stood there watching her, and it was hard to see what there was in his face. There was certainly disbelief in his voice. She didn't want sympathy, and there was none of that either.

'Yes,' she snapped. 'But I'm all right now, thank you.' She was fast regaining her confidence. She hated him knowing, but he did, and there was nothing she could do about it, but he wasn't going to have any satisfaction. 'I'll just tidy up and decide what we're having for dinner, then I'll go up top and to the beach.' She gave a practically silent final sniff, and stalked past him towards the refrigerator.

'Liar,' he said.

Donna whirled round. 'I *beg* your pardon?'

'I said you're a liar. You hadn't got a headache, you were just feeling as though the world was against you—so why not admit it?'

'It's nothing to do with you, that's why,' she retorted.

'I'll bet it has,' he said, and looked her up and down. 'No one's ever told you the truth before——'

'And does that make you feel pleased with yourself?' she cut in. 'Or are you so used to reducing women to tears that one more doesn't make any difference?'

She blinked hard, resisted the temptation to sniff again, and looked coldly at him. He walked over to her as she stood by the refrigerator.

'Neither,' he answered. 'I'm just surprised that you *could* feel sorry for yourself. I thought you'd be tougher than that. You a Webster girl—one of the charmed clan. I thought they bred you to be more resilient, to ride with the punches——'

'I'm not a boxer,' she snapped. 'And it's none of your business anyway. So why don't you just go and do whatever you're going to do up on deck and leave me alone?'

'That's better,' he remarked. 'You're fighting back now. Much better than sitting there crying your heart out—besides, it makes your eyes all pink.'

'Well, well,' she even managed a scornful laugh. 'You sure know how to make a girl feel good. I can understand *you* coming here on your own. I'll bet everyone avoids you like the plague wherever you go— and with your line of conversation, I'm not surprised!' Her cheeks glowed with temper, and when Brent began to laugh she had to clench her fists to stop herself from hitting him.

'Honey, you don't know the half of it,' he said when at last he could speak. 'But keep going—I find your insults very amusing.'

'I'm glad something amuses you!' she retorted.

He put his hand underneath her chin, and tilted it up so that he could look deeply into her eyes.

'*You* amuse me,' he said softly. 'You're a bundle of selfish emotions all wrapped up in a beautiful package—and what the hell Steven, the ardent pursuer sees in you I wouldn't know. But he's probably never looked beneath the surface.' He let her go abruptly. 'He very probably deserves you—and you him.' His face was no longer amused. 'Don't keep on feeling sorry for yourself while you're on board this ship, I don't like it. Snap out of it, get some work done—and we'll maybe get on better.'

'Don't worry—Captain,' she breathed. 'I'll do my share—while I'm here.'

'That's fine. Just remember it.'

They were facing each other, and tension, sudden and shocking, filled the small room; it sparked around them like a fine current of electricity that touched them both, and as their eyes met and clashed in a battle of wills, Donna knew that Brent was as aware of it as she. He was a powerful creature, all male, strong, tough, ruthless, and with a tongue as caustic as acid; she was smaller, weaker physically and emotionally, but fighting back, and she was all woman—and knew it. Her fine soft skin was prickling with the sharp tension and aggression that was so vivid it was almost tangible, and she saw his jaw tighten as he looked at her, saw the dark hardness of his face, and knew—just for a brief second—a startled sense of awareness. What had just happened, she didn't fully know. All she was conscious of, with every sense, was that Brent Sanders was suddenly aware of her as a woman, and not just a spoilt little rich girl.

She straightened her shoulders and stood up tall and proud, her eyes wide and dark with the realisation. She felt her heart beat faster, so that a pulse drummed in her throat, and she subconsciously put her hand to her neck, to conceal it. 'I'll remember it,' she answered slowly. She held his gaze. He wasn't going to look away, neither was she. There was a raw excitement in the air, and it was more than just a battle of wills now, it was a polarity, a kind of magnetism that stretched like a taut thread that might suddenly snap between them. Then, suddenly, something happened to her—and she could no longer look at him. She averted her face, and the spell was broken—and he walked out of the galley.

Donna's heart thudded so hard that she could feel it in every inch of her. 'Dear God,' she whispered, shaken, as she went over to the sink to bathe her face in clear cold water from the tap. She was still trembling with what had happened, with the shock of the sudden knowledge that had filled her and made her turn away lest he see. She had, in a moment of self-knowledge, known that she wanted him.

It had never happened to her before. Yet suddenly and inexplicably she had wanted to be held by him, and taken—she gasped as she splashed water over her head and face, and all was normal again. The absurd fancy—for that was all it had been—was gone for good. She even managed to laugh about it. Too ridiculous for words! She busied herself for the next few minutes deciding about food, concentrating hard, then went up on the deck. Of Brent there was no sign, although there was a lounging chair in the shade, and a pile of papers on it weighted with a stone. Donna climbed over the side, found a secluded spot out of sight of the boat, and lay down to drink in the sun. And to think.

It was only much later that evening that the disturbing memory of what had happened came back to Donna. Brent had gone for a swim after working and the boat was filled with light from galley and deck, and she was cleaning the galley as if her life depended on it, and almost enjoying it, when the image of his face as it had been when they had silently stood looking at each other during their clash came back to her. She paused in wiping down the stainless steel sink and looked out at the darkened night sky, and she was filled with warmth, almost a fire coursing through her veins. It was ridiculous to even think about, she told herself, but why then had the memory of the warmth returned too to fill her now? Many men had wanted to make love to her, and some had been more persistent than others, but none had affected her. Yet this man, who didn't even like her, certainly didn't desire her, had had a strange effect on her—admittedly only for a fleeting second, but it had been there. Perhaps, she thought, as she wiped busily at the sink, that's why. Just a contrary whim on my part, knowing he doesn't even remotely want me. Yes, that's what it was. Thus reassured, she dismissed the memory. Why, tomorrow she'd have a laugh about it—as long as Brent wasn't there to give her one of his cool mind-reading looks— that wouldn't do at all. He was far too shrewd.

She began to hum a little song to herself. It was nearly ten, and she was tired. She had sunbathed for a couple of hours, fallen asleep in the sun, then changed and had a refreshing swim. Brent had caught a large fish which she had cooked for dinner with vegetables, and the atmosphere had been almost civilised. It was by far the best way to be, of course. Life would be unbearable otherwise, and Donna had exerted herself to be calm, pleasant, talking about a visit to Mexico a few years previously because he had a Mexican primitive painting in the main cabin which she had admired, and after they had eaten she had read for a while and Brent had continued his paper work in his cabin until going for a swim.

He had a record-player and tape-recorder on board, and after finishing in the galley Donna went and put a record on in the main cabin, a larger room, comfortably furnished with dark brown settee and chairs, and a drinks cabinet, and the record-player. Here she settled herself and listened to soothing Tchaikovsky ballet music; she picked up her book and began to read it again.

The boat rocked slightly and she could hear Brent on deck, then his footsteps on the stair. His cabin door opened, then closed, and she concentrated on the thriller she was reading, and wondered if any of her family had given her a thought since leaving England. Probably not. They were all totally wrapped up in their own affairs; they all went their own ways, and always had done. Donna had accepted this because she knew no other way of life, and only winning counted, and being best at everything, and being seen in all the right places at the right times of year. Some friends were expecting her to join them on their yacht in Greece in a week or so, for a cruise round the Aegean Sea. When she didn't turn up they would phone someone else. . . .

Donna put her book down. That was it. That summed it up. People were dispensable. There was always someone else available, a new face, a new tan, a new name. It was a merry-go-round, and she had dared to step off it for a while. She wondered how long it would be before she stepped back on it—and as she did, Brent walked in. He wore jeans and black tee-shirt. Instantly Donna got to her feet. 'Do you want me to switch the record off?' she asked him.

'No, it's fine. Do you want a drink?'

'Yes, please.' She followed him to the drinks cabinet. He had told her to help herself, but she hadn't wanted to when he wasn't there. She was treading very warily with him, for reasons she didn't fully understand, except that it made life a lot easier. The emotional storm of the afternoon had taken its toll belatedly and she knew she couldn't face another battle—not yet.

'What will you have?' Brent stood aside to let her see the bottles and she pointed.

'Dry Martini. Shall I fetch the ice?'

'Please.' He began filling two glasses, Martini for her, whisky for himself, and Donna went to the galley. When she returned he was sitting in an easy chair opposite her settee. He held up his glass for her to put ice in. 'Thanks,' he said.

'Did you enjoy your swim?'

'It was all right.' The dark grey eyes were watchful. 'I'm turning in soon. You can stay up as long as you like, as long as you remember to turn the lights out when you go.'

'No, I'll go to bed when you do. I'm tired.' This would be her first night on board his boat. She had known him for a little over twenty-four hours, and she was sharing his boat with him. Yet she knew next to nothing about him, only his name, and that he was a treasure-hunter, an adventurer—and a loner. She didn't even know where he came from, or how old he was, or whether he had a family—or a wife. She looked into her glass, watching the ice rapidly melting, because it was easier than looking at him, because he saw too much.

Not only did he see too much, but he said things that no one else ever said. He spoke of things that were best left hidden, and she had never met a man like that before, and that too, as well as all the other things about him, was disturbing. He was watching her now; she sensed it, and, driven by a compulsion she could not resist, she looked up at last to meet his eyes; they were dark, unfathomable—like him. His face was expressionless. He was sipping his drink, his eyes upon her, over the rim of the glass, and Donna felt uneasy. No man ever watched her like this either. Open admiration—she was used to that, or lust—that too—but not the dark unreadable gaze that was more disturbing than anything else.

'Didn't anyone ever teach you it was bad manners to stare?' she asked him, keeping her tone deliberately light—something she wouldn't have made the effort to do if he had been anyone else.

'Frequently,' he answered dryly, 'but as you'll have noticed, I don't obey the normal rules of behaviour.'

There were answers she could have given, several, each one sharp, cutting—but she didn't. That much she had learned in a very short time. Brent's tongue could be more devastating than hers. She shrugged instead. 'I had noticed,' she said, equally dryly.

He finished his drink and stood up. 'I'm going to bed now,' he told her. 'Don't forget—lights out when you go. Goodnight, Donna.' He walked out and closed the door after him and she was alone again. That was it. Goodnight, and gone. She finished her drink, took both glasses out to rinse, checked that all the kitchen equipment was off, then went back into the main cabin, switched off the record-player and the lights and walked into her own cabin. She could hear Brent moving about in his, and for a few minutes she stood in the darkness of her own just listening to the quiet footsteps, a door opening, the shower running.

She crossed to the windows and looked out at the dark island and the sea beyond, glinting palely in the light from a yellow-white moon. Nothing stirred outside. It was a warm night, holding a reflection of the day's intense heat, yet it was pleasant to her skin. Donna undressed in the dark, then went for a shower in her minuscule shower cabin, seeing only by the moonlight which streamed through the porthole. She had been on many boats. This was not as luxurious as most, but it was well fitted and compact and comfortable. She was used to opulence, and extravagance, in her surroundings. She had been brought up to expect—and be sure of receiving—the best wherever she went in the world, with or without her family. She would not have normally slept in a cabin without air-conditioning—but here there was none. The plane had been hot the previous night, this could be just as much so. It didn't appear to bother Brent, as his only comment about it had been that she would soon get used to sleeping in heat—said with the merest trace of amusement, no more.

She heard his window being opened, padding footsteps, the creak of his bed, then silence. Donna, restless with something she didn't understand, went over to her own window and looked out again. The moon cut a path in the sea, a path of silver, trembling, scintillating, haunting. It was as if it lured her, to walk out, to go along it, to find—what to find? She turned away, wide awake, and looked round the darkened, unfamiliar cabin. Shadows mocked her, she felt very much alone. While only yards away, the unknown man called Brent Sanders lay in his bed. Was he wide awake too? Or was he already asleep? There were no sounds now from his cabin. The only noise came from the faint slap of the water against the boat, the only movement from the sea itself, an imperceptible rocking. Donna took a deep breath and went to lie down, covering herself with the thin sheet, lying on her back, eyes open. Pictures of her life came into her mind, brief distorted scenes flashing past as on an old film. Restlessly she turned, resolutely closing her eyes to shut them out, replacing them with images of that morning's diving, seeing herself moving through the darkened world underwater, following her companion, the one who had told her that he didn't want her with him again.

'I don't care,' she whispered fiercely into the dark, but she did. The words seemed to echo softly in the heavy night air; don't care, don't care——

When she opened her eyes, surprised at having slept at all, her pillow was damp with tears and the dream that had left her shaken and trembling and afraid was vivid in her mind. She sat up, gasping deep breaths at the memories, still painful and raw. She had been underwater in the ship, only Brent had gone, his mocking laughter fading away as he had swum off to leave her trapped in a dark cell full of weirdly shaped creatures that swam round her, touching her, pushing her. She had been afraid, and had called out for him, but only the laughter remained in that mocking echo, that filled her head and made her think it would burst. The perspiration ran down her face and she wiped it, then lay back, relief gradually replacing the panic as it was eased away.

'Donna?' The door opened silently, and he stood there, a shadowy figure with the light streaming in behind him. She blinked at the sudden blaze of yellow. 'What the hell's the matter now?' He came in, and the door swung to behind him, not quite shutting, but leaving only a narrow gap.

'Did I shout?'

'I wouldn't have come here if you hadn't,' he answered dryly, and crossed to the bed. 'What is it?'

'I had a nightmare.'

He grunted something and half turned away. 'Well, for God's sake keep it quieter if you have another one,' he said, with no trace of sympathy—not that she would have expected any from *him*. 'I need *my* sleep.'

'I didn't do it on purpose,' she retorted.

Brent regarded her levelly from the doorway. 'No, I don't suppose you did,' he answered. 'It doesn't make you any the less noisy.'

'May I go and make myself a drink?' she asked, knowing she would find sleep difficult again, after that.

'Feel free. Try to make it quietly, though. It's nearly three o'clock in the morning.'

He went out leaving the door ajar, and Donna waited a moment, then slid out of bed. She wore nothing, and grabbed her thin cotton wrap, belting it securely before venturing out into the passageway. Brent's door was open, but his cabin was in darkness. She felt the merest prickle of unease as she walked past it, as though he might be lurking in the darkness, to pounce on her like one of those nameless, shapeless horrors that had haunted her dreams. But there was no sound, no movement. She filled the kettle and put tea in the pot. Nothing, but nothing, was as good as a cup of tea at times of stress. It had always been Nonie's remedy, and the memory was a soothing one to Donna as she poured out the tea, added lemon juice, and caried the cup back to her cabin. There she sat on her bed in the dark and sipped the hot refreshing drink.

'What did you make?' His voice carried clearly in the dark, a deep voice, and powerful, like him.

'Lemon tea,' she answered.

'Any left in the pot?' She was surprised by the question, but hers not to reason why, hers to humour.

'Yes. I'll get you one.' She put her cup down, switched the companionway light on again, and scurried along to the galley.

She carried the steaming mug back, tapped perfunctorily on his open door, and went in. He sat up, naked under the sheet as far as she could judge, not that she was going to examine too closely, and she handed him the tea. 'Sit down,' he invited.

Donna remained standing. 'No, I don't think so,' she answered.

'I said—sit down.'

'Why?'

'Well, I'm not going to attack you, if that's what's troubling your pretty head. I merely want to talk.'

'At three o'clock in the morning?'

'It seems as good a time as any, considering I was thoroughly awakened by your screams ten minutes ago.'

'Screams? Did I scream? I thought I'd shouted.'

'You gave several bloodcurdling screams. I thought you were being murdered!'

'Which is, no doubt, why you *charged* in so swiftly?'

she rejoined, remembering the silent way he had entered.

'*If* you had been,' he shot back, 'there would have been no sense in alerting any attacker—though God knows, I should have had more sense than to imagine anyone *else* could possibly be here. However, at that time of night, and freshly torn from a deep sleep, my reasoning faculties weren't in top gear.'

'Your tongue is,' she answered caustically.

'I never lose my ability to deal with inanities,' he rejoined. 'You'd do well to remember that, it'll save you a lot of grief.'

'I'll get my tea,' she said, and went out. When she returned she sat primly right at the foot of the bed. 'Well?' she said.

'May I borrow your plane for a few hours?'

'Can you fly?'

'I wouldn't be asking if I couldn't, would I?'

She was confused, not as wide awake as she had thought. Did he mean now? And for what purpose? 'I suppose so,' she answered. 'When?'

'Tomorrow. Or should I say later today? I can see the next question positively trembling on your lips, so I'll save you asking. I need some more equipment— not essential stuff, but something that would make my task easier. I don't want my boat spotted round here yet—and your plane would be perfectly anonymous, for my purposes. It is hired, isn't it?'

'Yes. Where are you taking it?'

'La Barra—about fifty miles away from here. There's a very good store there with diving equipment. I'll only be gone a few hours in all.'

'Can I come with you?' The question surprised

Donna herself, even as she asked it. It apparently had the same effect on him.

'Why?' he asked bluntly. 'I thought you came here to escape from the world, not to rejoin it so soon.'

'It *is* my plane,' she answered tartly. 'And I—need some things.'

'As you say, it's yours. I want to leave early, say eight. Will that suit you?'

'Yes.' She stood up. 'If that's all, I'll go back to my bed.'

'That's all. Goodnight.' Brent lifted his beaker. 'Thanks for the tea.'

'You're welcome. It's yours anyway.' Donna moved smartly away from his bed, from his all-maleness. She found him disturbing and she didn't know why. Perhaps it was because he, of practically all the men she had met within the past few years, seemed generally immune to her attractions. She expected— and got—a very different reaction from males. She was used to admiring glances, smouldering looks that made no doubt about their owner's interest and intentions. She accepted it; it was sometimes, after all, very amusing, a little game to play. But he didn't look at her as though he was bowled over. There was almost exasperation occasionally in the way he regarded her, as though she were a nuisance of a child, someone to be tolerated—but only just. It was frustrating and infuriating, and there was absolutely nothing she could do about it.

This is ridiculous! Donna thought. It was scarcely seven, yet she had awoken minutes before from a deep sleep to find herself completely and instantly wide awake, heart beating fast in anticipation. She sat up in bed and looked at the sunlight streaming in through her small square window. She was going to La Barra, with Brent, and the thought was a delicious one. She put her hand to her head. I *am* mad, she decided, quite crazy. I've been here two days, a virtual prisoner—and I'm as excited as a child at the thought of a trip out! Then realisation dawned. It was *he* who had said he was keeping her there—yet he had agreed to let her go back to civilisation with him. That didn't make sense.

Further sleep was out of the question now. She got out of bed, turned on the water, took her shampoo in with her and enjoyed a brief cool shower, coming out towel-clad, her hair dripping down her back. She heard a noise outside her door, then:

'Donna? You awake?'

She made sure the towel was securely fastened and called out: 'Yes, come in.'

He was dressed in shorts and white tee-shirt. Freshly shaved and with black hair as wet as hers, he walked in, took a long steady look at her and said: 'You should have told me you weren't respectable.'

'I thought you already knew,' she retorted flippantly. 'I didn't think it would bother you.'

'It doesn't.' His voice was devoid of any expression—unlike his eyes. There was a trace in them of something she had only glimpsed briefly at the pool the previous day. It had been disturbing then; it was equally so now.

She took a deep breath. 'Why—why are you letting me go with you?' she asked quickly. Brent had turned already, as if to go out, but he paused, didn't turn round.

'I'll see you in the galley when you're dressed,' he

answered. 'We'll talk there.' He went out and closed the door after him. Donna stared hard at it as if it might answer the tumbling questions in her brain.

And damn you too, she thought. Something had made him—no, not exactly angry, not that, but—different. She didn't like it. She didn't want anything to spoil things; he might refuse to let her go. She found clean pants, shorts and sun-top and dressed in moments, then she rubbed her hair quickly with the towel and went along to the galley. It was immediately evident that he had been up for a while. The kettle was boiling, toast was already made and on a plate on the table together with butter and apricot conserve. He turned and glanced at her briefly from the sink.

'I'm dressed, as you see,' she told him.

'Yes. Sit down, breakfast's ready.'

'Is that what you came to tell me?'

'Yes.'

'And are you going to answer the question?'

'Which one?' He put two cups on the table, and filled the teapot.

Donna bit back irritation, her feelings mixed. Brent had the power to make her unsure of herself and she definitely didn't like it—and there was nothing she could do about it, which was even worse. He could easily tell her the trip was off, and she didn't want that to happen, not one bit.

'Why are you letting me go?'

'As you said, it's your plane.' He sat opposite her at the table and regarded her very levelly across it. The disturbing look—the one she didn't understand—had gone, and in its place something else equally puzzling. There was, no doubt about it, a difference in him this morning.

'But suppose I tell—I thought you didn't——' she

was stumbling, fumbling for words. Inwardly she wanted to scream. What on earth's the matter with me? she wondered. 'I thought——'

'You thought I didn't trust you?' he finished for her, and smiled, but the smile didn't quite reach his eyes. 'Is that what you're trying to say?'

She gritted her teeth. 'Yes.'

'You've obviously not been to La Barra. It's hardly the hub of the universe—and I can't really see you rushing up to the nearest local and telling him you're being kept prisoner on an island fifty miles south-west by a madman who's looking for treasure—can you?'

Donna didn't answer, merely looked stonily back at him. 'Besides,' he added, voice soft, 'I don't think you do want to escape any more, do you?'

She took a deep breath. There would have been an instant—devastating retort on her lips only yesterday. Now, at his words, at what she had, she supposed, *known* he was going to say, she knew the deep truth of them. She shrugged. She could not, for the moment, answer. Nor did Brent seem to expect her to. He poured out two cups of tea, handed her one silently, took a piece of toast and began to butter it.

No, she thought. Oh no, I don't want to escape any more. And she didn't know why, she only knew that it was a fact. She reached out for the toast, her hand shaking. She tried desperately to hide the tremor, praying he wouldn't notice, but he was not looking at her any more, he was fishing a speck of dirt out of the conserve. He was concentrating on that. She could scarcely breathe. It was as though there were no air in the room, and she felt stifled. She glanced desperately at the closed window, then jumped up, unable to sit still any longer, and opened it.

'I—it's too warm.' Her words broke the spell that had held them both. Brent looked up then, and a muscle moved in his jaw, and his eyes had gone dark, very dark and shadowed.

'You didn't answer my question,' he stated.

'I—don't mind staying.'

'That's not an answer.'

'It's all you'll get!' Spirit returned. She could look at him now. The moments of intolerable, endless tension had passed. A brief madness, a sudden strangeness that had knocked her almost dizzy, but now was gone. Donna had regained her confidence.

'Then I'll have to keep an eye on you, won't I?' His tone was deliberately light, yet she sensed an effort behind it.

'I give you my word I won't do anything stupid.'

She met his gaze, and the brief eye contact was quite startling.

He nodded. 'That'll do.' He looked away from her, and at his watch. 'As we're both ready, I suggest we leave in a few minutes. I've replaced the part I removed, by the way.'

'Oh. When?' It was easier to talk naturally. And better kept this way too.

'Earlier—before I——' he hesitated for a second, 'came in to see if you were awake.'

'Oh, then. Yes, I see.'

There was something else she had to ask, and it might as well be now, then if he said no, it wouldn't hurt by the time they reached La Barra. 'Brent, you say you're going to a store that sells diving equipment?'

'Yes?' Eyes on her, questioning eyes. He knew, he knew. She was going to take the plunge anyway.

'If—they've got a diving suit to fit me, may I——'
deep breath. *Now.* 'May I dive again with you? I want
to—and I'll do *exactly* as you tell me.' Her hands were
clasped together on her lap so tightly that her nails
dug into the skin.

'I believe you would,' he answered. 'We'll see, shall
we, if they have?' Then he smiled, very slightly. 'I do
believe you're learning.'

CHAPTER FIVE

LA BARRA was a much larger island than the one they had just left. Donna remembered passing it on her way south from Barbados, and it was almost in direct line between the two places. It had a thriving fishing industry, was a visiting place for cruise liners, and had a fascinating market place that sold everything from island lace to lobsters, from pearl necklaces to grandfather clocks. There were two large hotels, several seafood restaurants and many excellent food shops. Donna intended to visit at least one to replenish their food supplies, and told Brent so as they approached the large curving bay already dotted with fishing boats, small yachts, and one other seaplane. They were losing height now, sweeping round in an arc that would position them most accurately at the refuelling depot at the tip of the peninsular at one end of the bay.

'Good idea. If you see any decent prawns, get some, will you?'

'I will.' The journey had been surprisingly pleasant, no undertones of anything to disturb or dismay. If he was exerting himself to be nice it was working. And Donna responded, not consciously aware of doing so, but finding herself more relaxed, for the moment, than she had been for quite a while. For longer, in fact, than she could remember. She didn't question it, she accepted.

'We'll leave the plane by the depot and have it

refuelled before we return,' he told her. 'We'll walk from there, go to the marine store and then split up—you do your shopping, I'll do mine.'

'Oh.' She nodded. 'Fine.' It seemed so much easier to agree—for the moment anyway.

Brent guided the plane in, there was a bump as they hit water, then he was coasting along, nearer, nearer to the depot—a large rambling Nissen hut with ramshackle extensions that proudly proclaimed itself to be 'La Barra International Marine Works' in large red letters on a white plasterboard background. A Barranian in blue overalls leaned against the wall and watched their approach, sunglasses hiding his eyes, a stub of unlit cigar at the corner of his mouth. He appeared to be chewing something as well.

'And thank God his cigar's unlit,' murmured Brent. He climbed out of the cockpit on to an equally ramshackle—to match the building, no doubt—wooden jetty, and leaned down to help Donna up. She passed him her large blue tote bag first, then grasped his hand and was yanked up with no ceremony to stand beside him.

'Thanks,' she murmured. The man had vanished, presumably into the building, and another, older man had come out to peer at them. Similarly clad, in blue overalls, he was whistling tunelessly, and nodded amiably as they passed by him.

'Nice day,' he called.

'Yes, lovely,' Brent agreed.

'You want fuel, then, sir?'

'We do indeed, in a couple of hours.'

'No problem, sir, we'll be here.'

The man nodded again and shambled, still whistling, back into the building. Beyond lay the town, houses and shops clustered round the main square with its already crowded market place, the two hotels aloof on higher ground at the back, overlooking square, and bay, and sea. Palm trees and colourful flowering bushes lent added colour to an already colourful island, and Donna suddenly thought, as she and Brent made their way towards the market—I'm enjoying this. Never before had she seen a place so bright and cheerful, and she had been to many similar. Today there was something different, an added dimension, a clarity that made everything seem sharper and clearly defined. How strange, she thought, and didn't realise why.

The roads were badly paved, but there were few cars, the main transport being by bicycle or horse-drawn carriage—with the occasional single-decker bus to add variety. People milled round them now, and they could see the nearer stalls set out, and scents of pineapple and melon mingled with heavier spices to tease the taste-buds and stimulate the appetite, and Donna realised that she was hungry.

'Can we eat here?' she asked. A sudden impulse really, that, as were the words that followed, out before she thought about them: 'My treat.'

Brent looked down at her, grabbed her arm and pulled her to him just in time to save her from being sent flying by a youth on a garishly painted bicycle. 'I can hardly refuse an offer like that,' he responded.

'Then we'll meet after our separate shopping, shall we?'

'There's a good seafood bar next door—or nearly—to my store,' he told her. He steered her to the left, between two rows of stalls. Their pace had slowed considerably owing to the dense tide of humanity swirling round. Bidding was brisk at the pot stall, and a crowd hung round listening to the bargains being advertised by a fast-talking Barranian. It was just like Petticoat Lane, Donna thought, bemused, and laughed—and when he asked if it was a private joke, she told him why. Brent looked down at her. For a moment they were pressed close together by the mass of bodies, and he put out his arms in a protective gesture round her—and she suddenly knew why she was enjoying herself, and tried to move away from him, but it was impossible. They were at the very core of the market, and centre of the throng, and La Barra might not be the hub of the universe as Brent had said, but at that moment it felt like it. Snatches of several languages teased their ears. A fat German called to his wife. He'd either had his pocket picked or found a bargain, it was difficult to tell; two French girls pushed past arguing volubly about a necklace; an American laden with cameras assured his wife that yes, goddammit, he'd remembered to get film, didn't she ever listen?

And right in the middle of this incredible hubbub Brent eased a breathless Donna along, his hands on her shoulders and she with trembling legs because strange things were happening to her, unknown sensations filling her and she still didn't know why.

Then, at last, they emerged from the thick of it into comparative peace. They were through the market, they could walk separately, and did, and he might never have touched her. But the memory lingered. Her shoulders still bore the imprint of his hands; the flesh tingled. She took a deep breath.

She looked back to the colourful sea of bodies moving, swaying, shuffling slowly in a gentle wave of humanity, then at Brent. 'Amazing, isn't it?' he said. 'People *en masse*. Bet you've never done that before.'

'Done what?'

'Pushed your way through a crowd like that.'

Donna thought for a second. She didn't need to really; of course she hadn't. She wouldn't have dreamt of mingling with tourists and islanders in any kind of market. Why should she? Websters were different. And she knew why he had done it—of course she knew. 'No, I haven't,' she answered. 'Is that why we went?'

He nodded, 'I thought you'd like to see how the other half lives.' But it was humour that lay behind his words, not sarcasm. She counted to five very slowly. Today, she was *not* going to spoil anything.

'It was very interesting.'

'You said that as though you meant it.' She stopped walking. They were outside one of the many food shops anyway, it was perfectly natural to stop, and look.

'I'm not going to rise to any bait today, Brent,' she said evenly, and looked at him, and kept a pleasant smile on her face. He mustn't spoil it either, she thought—oh, please don't let him. Let's have a truce for one day at least, because much to my surprise I'm enjoying it, and I haven't really enjoyed anything in a very long time. And perhaps he saw something in her eyes, a silent unspoken plea. For long seconds he regarded her, and he was puzzled, she knew that. She felt tears rise at the back of her throat and blinked quickly before they should show. . . .

People passed them, no one pushing now, or needing to, no one looking save in mild interest at the two tall strangers, and they might have been alone

there, there might have been no one else anywhere
near. A golden, shimmering invisible thread stretched
between them in an instant, and neither moved;
although they could not see it, they knew it was there.
She saw his face change in that awareness; something
had reached out from her to him, as old as time,
nothing that could ever be spoken or acknowledged
but as deep and primitive as life itself; the essence.

He stood there, unmoving, yet it hit him with the
force of a blow; Donna was aware of that deep down
within herself. This large, extremely powerful male
responded; almost as if unknowing what he was doing,
Brent lifted his hand to her cheek, touched, very
lightly, the skin beneath her eye, looked at the
teardrop that glistened on his finger as if he had never
seen one before, like a man in a trance, then put his
hand down again by his side.

All this had happened within the space of a few
moments. But they had been moments out of time as
though it had expanded within a small secret bubble;
as though it could have been for an eternity, and
nothing would ever be the same again, for either of
them. The gossamer-winged moment was gone. Brent
bowed his head fractionally, and the spell was broken.
That brief acknowledgment was all that was needed.
Nothing would—or could—ever be said about what
had passed, for there were no words that could express
anything so raw and primeval.

Donna, feeling as though she were emerging from
somewhere rich and strange, touched his arm. 'Where
is this store we're going to?' she asked gently.

His eyes focussed again on her. 'Three—four
minutes' walk from here,' he answered. It was as if he
had snapped out of a trance. 'Just beyond that bus.'

She looked, saw the ancient green bus disgorging passengers, wanted to laugh, but couldn't. Wanted to cry, but wouldn't. 'Ah yes,' she said, 'I see.'

They walked on. Nothing had happened. It was forgotten in an instant. It would not be remembered, for how could it be? It went too deep for that.

The wet-suit was tried on, and it fitted, and was left to be packed up together with various tools that Brent had bought, and collected by them later. Outside the shop they stood on the pavement and he looked at his watch. 'Will two hours do you?' he asked.

'Yes,' Donna nodded.

'And we'll meet back inside there——' he pointed to the restaurant near them. A large wooden lobster loomed over the doorway, painted an improbable shade of pink.

'At two-thirty, yes.' She checked her watch with his. 'I want clothes shops. Any ideas?'

'Keep straight on. Turn right, and go up and back round towards the Balmoral Hotel. There are a few boutiques, I think—nothing very fancy, though.'

She shrugged. 'That's okay. I'm only going window-shopping—well, perhaps. I'll see you later, here.'

'Yes. Don't forget if you see any——'

'Prawns—I haven't forgotten. 'Bye.' She set off, hitching her tote-bag higher. When she reached the corner, Brent had gone. Light of step, and heart, she set off walking up the sloping and gently curving street with its many shops. Not as populated here; tourists and islanders alike were, in the main, enjoying the delights of the market, but there were sufficient people to make her walk interesting, and not enough to feel crowded. The sun blazed relentlessly down from a white sky and her shorts and top clung to her in the high humidity. She stopped for a cool lime drink at a pavement café, and watched the passers-by as she sipped it. She had an hour and forty minutes. Time enough to look at dresses and be back at the Improbable Lobster, as she had christened the restaurant, in good time for Brent. She had no deep thoughts in her head, content just to watch and be watched in return, sip her cool drink, study an insect that had landed on her table and was busy drinking from a small puddle of spilled coffee—or tea—it could have been either. It was fascinating to speculate. Tea or coffee? With or without sugar? Did the insect know—or care—which? It was extremely difficult, so hot was the day, to bring her mind to anything else more complex.

The drink finished, the insect departed for different delights at perhaps some other café. Donna walked on, discovered the first boutique, and went in. She bought a turquoise swimsuit and a pair of rope-soled sandals, carried on to the next shop where she fell for—and also bought—a delightful dress in swirly green chiffon. Her tote-bag was beginning to bulge. From a chemist she bought shampoo and sun-tan oil and then looking at her watch discovered she had only ten minutes to get back to the restaurant, which was fortunately downhill all the way. She was just in time. Brent was walking in as she turned the corner, he too package-laden. He hadn't seen her. She hurried her steps to catch him up. It seemed important that she shouldn't keep him waiting.

They reached Paradise Island after an uneventful

journey home, and it was early evening. On board the boat again Brent said: 'If you're going to prepare dinner, I have some work to do in my study. Don't hurry anything, I'll be an hour or two.'

'I've bought the ingredients for a special sauce to go with the prawns, and we'll have it with hot vegetables—I bought those too. Okay?'

He nodded as he went out of the galley. 'I'll leave it to you entirely.'

Donna pulled a face after him. What had she expected? That he would fall on his knees in rapture? Some chance of that, she reflected wryly as she began to stow the perishable food in the refrigerator. For a few hours, on La Barra, he had been a different man, more relaxed.

They had been the happiest hours she had spent in a very long time. Now, home again—how strange, she mused, I call it home—it was the other Brent; as if La Barra had been a brief holiday for him too, but life was far too serious for frivolity.

She began to peel potatoes, wondering, but only briefly, what her two sisters would think if they could see her now. That she was undoubtedly mad. The thought of anything approaching domestic chores had always filled them with horror. Me too, she thought, as she dug eyes out of a particularly large potato, but then they're not here and I am. She was absolutely determined to do for them both the most superb meal Brent had ever eaten. She knew what his opinion of her was, knew also—this thought with a wry inner smile—what was hers of him. A state of brittle truce existed, had almost from their first startling encounter—but her senses were alive, attuned. She *felt* more alive than she had for ages, her mind abuzz with ideas and images. She remembered their walk through the crowded market place, how everything had seemed more brightly coloured, how sharply aware she had been of her surroundings. Markets were vulgar places, best avoided, or skirted as quickly as possible if there were no alternative—but he had been right, she conceded reluctantly, he had shown her something alien to her special world, and she had found it fascinating.

And more surprises over lunch. Brent knew his wines; he had ordered the one palatable one she had noticed on an exceedingly limited wine list, had chosen for them a superb lobster dish, the memory of which still lingered and had made the lunch memorable. She knew next to nothing about him—but she was beginning to find out by a very gradual process that the man with whom she was reluctantly sharing an island had far greater depths to him than could be discerned in any simple way. He had not allowed her to pay for the meal, had simply said: 'Next time,' cryptically in answer to Donna's protests. Did that mean he planned to go there again? She wouldn't ask, of course, but—the thought lingered, and was a pleasant speculation.

She tipped the giant prawns into a bowl of water and began to shell them. No easy task this, one that needed care and concentration. With the prawns she intended giving Brent—and herself—courgettes fried in butter, and she had also bought a wholemeal loaf with which to make garlic bread. She mentally uttered a small prayer of thanks for her two years at finishing school. She had attended cookery classes with the greatest reluctance—*she* would never need to cook anything!—had paid the minimum attention, but was now quietly grateful for her excellent memory. This meal would be a challenge—and she found it becoming more important to her with every minute that passed. Brent thought her pretty useless—he had made that eminently clear on more than one occasion in their brief acquaintanceship. She was going to show him he was wrong. And in the morning, when they dived, he would see a different Donna as well. She lifted her chin, standing straight-backed and tall, and looked out of the window at the beautiful island before her. Nonie hadn't let her down, telling her to come here, and when she returned to Barbados she would tell her so.

She was thirsty. So too, most probably, was Brent. She had been vaguely aware of tapping sounds from what seemed like a distance, and had assumed he was using a typewriter. She had not been in the cabin he referred to as his study. He hadn't offered to show her, Donna had not been curious. She opened a carton of orange juice, poured two glasses full, picked one up and, carrying it, tapped on the closed door leading off from the galley. The tapping stopped.

'Come in,' Brent called, and Donna, admittedly slightly curious now, walked in—and stopped, her mouth opening in sheer overwhelming astonishment. She could not utter a word, so great was her surprise. 'You've brought me a drink, I see,' said Brent, not amused, not quite, but eyes with a slight trace of something she was scarcely aware of. 'How kind. Put it down on the desk, will you?'

'But—but——' she began, and gestured helplessly. He stood up, came over and took the glass from her.

'Before you drop it,' he explained in almost kindly tones. 'Never seen a study before?'

She had not expected anything like this. What had she expected? A desk, chair, typewriter, papers. Yes, that. The room she had entered had those, but it had infinitely more. Along the entire right wall was a computer surrounded by grey metal file drawers. The computer was a large impressive one, and flickering figures covered the screen—and the typewriter she had heard clicking was not the one on his desk, but the one in the computer bank. He turned away, pressed a key, and the screen blanked out. Then he turned back to her. 'Thanks for the drink,' he said. 'Just what I needed. If you don't mind, I am rather busy——' the words he left unspoken were delicately implied—so please go.

'I—yes, of course——' Donna began to back towards the door, quite unable to take her eyes from that blank silent screen.

'Careful you don't fall!'

She turned and went out, still feeling as if something had hit her on the head. Something with as much impact as a sandbag. She knew something about computers. Her father too had one installed in his London home and in their villa outside Nice, to keep in constant touch with his many business concerns. Donna had never given them a second thought, why should she? But to see one, so similar, here, had been a shock. It was so totally unexpected. It caused her to look round the galley with new eyes, seeing everything as it were from a fresh angle. She had never seen the boat in motion, of course, but the thought struck her that it must have a pretty powerful generator to cope with the electricity needed for such a complicated apparatus. She had thought the vessel ordinary, but it wasn't. She had assumed that Brent couldn't afford the luxury of air-conditioning. It now seemed as if that would be by choice, for the power needed to run that would be a mere fraction of what was needed to house and run a computer such as she had just seen in action.

She looked round her, and realised, very belatedly, what she should have observed before. The galley was superbly fitted—but with no trace of ostentation. That was the difference she had mistaken for economy. She closed her eyes. Brent had effectively demonstrated something to her by his very lack of interest in her surprise. He had no need to impress *anyone*. He was a man who didn't give a damn for others' approval or opinions. It was a sobering thought to have.

Donna, still slightly shaken, began to prepare the other vegetables.

The table was ready. Plates warmed in the small space at the bottom of the oven inside which foil-wrapped garlic bread heated beside a simmering casserole dish of prawns in a rich herb and butter sauce. The vegetables, cooked to perfection, were being kept at the right temperature on a pan of water. Donna washed her hands, looked round to make a final check, then went to Brent's study door. Hand lifted to tap on it, she was halted by the sound of his voice, and stopped, fearing to interrupt if he were talking on the radio telephone—another feature she had noted during her dizzying few moments in there.

His voice was low as if he preferred not to be overheard, but she found herself unable to move—and when she did, it was too late, for the next moment the door was flung open.

'I thought I heard someone outside.' Brent glared

down at her from his great height. 'Taken up eavesdropping now, have you?'

'No! I came to tell you that——'

'You didn't *knock*!'

'I was just about to when I thought—you were speaking on the radio—I didn't want to interrupt——'

His face softened fractionally, but not enough. Still hard, he stared at her as if seeking the truth of what she said, then he made a small sound deep in his throat and nodded slightly. She met his eyes with contempt, hers showing her feelings. 'If it was *that* private,' she snapped, 'you should have asked me to wait in my cabin. *I* can't help your study being next door to the galley!'

'Temper,' he warned. 'I've already told you——'

'Oh, go to hell!' Donna turned on her heel and marched away, but didn't get far, just inside her room, before he caught her arm and swung her round to face him. Before she could even begin to struggle he shook her, only slightly, but it was enough. 'Let me *go* at once!' she demanded hotly.

'I may have been mistaken——'

'You bloody well were!'

'But,' he went on as though she hadn't interrupted, 'but you will not lose your temper with *me*, *Miss* Webster, remember that.'

'Oh, I'll remember that!' she spat. 'I don't have much choice, do I?'

'Meaning?'

'I'm still a prisoner,' she shot back. 'I still can't leave, even if I wanted to. And I don't give a damn who you talk to on your radio—I couldn't care less! I came to tell you your dinner was ready and I've worked damned hard for the past *two* hours, and all you can do is accuse me of——' she sniffed. She was behaving like a two-year-old, and to her horror, she couldn't do anything about it. Her dinner, her lovely dinner that she had so wanted, so needed to impress him with—tears filled her eyes. He blurred, moved in a blur, and the next moment his lips came down on hers, warm, sweet and hard.

CHAPTER SIX

'Now. Shut up,' said Brent, and tipped his hand under her chin. Donna was—for the second time in two hours—speechless. He tapped her cheek. 'Right, let's go and eat this nectar from the gods. Just give me one minute to wash my hands and face and I'll be there.' With that he was gone. Donna stared after him, indignation vying with anger—and something else. Something infinitely sweet and disturbing; an echo of what had taken place outside a baker's shop returning to tantalise so briefly that it was gone before it could take shape.

Her lips tingled in the aftermath of his kiss. He had done it simply to silence her, and very effective it had been—and it had had not the slightest effect on him, that was obvious. But it had on Donna. She touched her mouth, rubbed her lips gently, wondered why it should have. Brent had kissed her before, as a simple alternative to striking her back after she had hit him. He had kissed her now for a different reason—and it *had* been different, but in what way she couldn't define.

She went into her shower cubicle, ran the tap, and rinsed her face in the water. Other memories surfaced, further back memories, disturbing ones. She had no idea why, now, she pushed them away from her and almost ran into the galley. No! She must not think of it—of *that*. No reason to, no reason at all, ever again. But Brent saw her face as she went in. He was waiting for her, this big shaggy-haired man with shrewd and all-seeing grey eyes who could kiss women and forget it instantly.

'What's the matter now?' he asked, frowning.

'Nothing. Nothing at all.' Don't look at me. Look away—let me get the dinner. Everything will be all right. It must be, it must be. The memories of a frightened twelve-year-old girl had no place here because this man had kissed her. 'Sit down, I'll dish up dinner——'

He did so, his question unanswered. He would forget in a moment, and so would Donna. Or would she? Would she *ever* really forget?

She concentrated on the task at hand. Everything had to be just right. Timing was everything. Garlic bread out first, on a plate. 'Please loosen the foil, will you? There's a knife to cut it with when we're ready.' Then the prawns, still in the casserole dish, to be set on the mat at the centre of the table. 'Careful, it's hot.' She put it down, uncovered the vegetables, and the pain the memories had brought with it was fading, couldn't for the moment compete with the fine concentration she needed if all were to be perfect.

'There.' Potatoes, butter-golden, courgettes a rich crisp brown, and she lifted the casserole lid, and Brent sniffed deeply and said one simple word.

'Beautiful.'

They were too. Everything was. The delicate bouquet of the herbs she had used blended a delicate flavour to sauce and prawns. There was enough and more to spare, and seeing his face as he looked at the dish, Donna spooned him a second helping, ignoring his not very convincing protests.

When they had at last finished he told her it was the most delicious meal he had eaten for a long time, and she believed him. And those other memories went away, almost as though they had never been.

Brent insisted on making the coffee and clearing the plates away. He then vanished, leaving the coffee to percolate—real ground coffee this time, not instant—and returned with a bottle of Benedictine and two liqueur glasses. Donna couldn't help smiling. It seemed a fitting end to what she had to admit had been a meal worthy of her efforts. She would probably tell Nonie about it when she returned. When she returned. . . . It came to her with the shock of a blow. Soon they would both leave the island and go their separate ways. Goodbye Donna, goodbye Brent. She would climb into her plane, and as it banked and climbed she would take one last look, and he might be standing there to wave to her, or he might already be on his way, the white boat speeding over the water, he at the controls and not giving any backward glances. She looked down at his packet of cigars on the table, lighter on top. And where would he go from there? And who had he been talking to so quietly on the radio? And why, for God's sake *why*, she thought, does it all matter so much?

'Coffee black?' His voice came as an intrusion.

'Oh. Yes, please.'

He seated himself comfortably, long legs spread out in front of him. 'You know, we could sit in the main cabin and have these.'

'I'm fine here,' she answered. The atmosphere was just right, perfectly civilised after a fine dinner. She didn't want it to change—not yet. This was precious. She watched him pour a good measure of Benedictine into each glass, watched the steam rising from the coffee cups, saw him take a cheroot and light it.

'Tomorrow I'd like to start diving early,' he told her.

'How early? Seven?'

'If you can manage that, yes.'

'I'll manage.'

'No food before we go down, for obvious reasons, and only a sip of coffee—for practical ones.'

'Yes, of course. How near do you think you are?'

'Hard to tell. I'll know better when I've taken a few more photos and developed them.'

'Here? You can develop them here?' More surprises.

Brent nodded. 'It won't take long. Then I can compare them with the plan of the boat. It's extremely difficult to know exactly where I'm hacking away at sometimes—the drill I bought today will be a big help.'

It was time for the big one, the one she really wanted to know more than anything else. 'When do you estimate you'll find what you're looking for?' She held her breath, scarcely aware of doing so.

He shrugged, eyed her shrewdly, as if assessing the probable length of time—as if, also, assessing her reasons. 'It could be another two or three weeks,' he answered. 'Why do you ask?'

She let out her breath—silently. 'I just wondered.'

'Really? You have more than just a passing curiosity in your voice.' He smiled faintly. 'Wondering about the length of your "imprisonment"?'

It was Donna's turn to shrug. She was quite pleased with it; a graceful, careless kind of movement. 'I'm in no hurry to go anywhere else,' she answered.

'Aren't the bright lights calling?' The faint edge of

mockery that tinged his words was better ignored. Instead she looked calmly across the table at him.

'What bright lights?' she queried. 'When you get too near, they cease to be bright.'

'Which is, of course,' he said very softly, 'one of the many reasons, apart from him-who-shall-be-nameless, that you wanted to get away.'

'We've been over this before.' She moved in her seat, uneasy. Don't let this be spoiled, please don't let it be——

'And where will you go when you leave here?'

'Back to Barbados to return the plane and see my godmother. Where will *you* go?'

'To London.'

'With the gold?'

He smiled faintly. 'Always supposing I find any, yes.'

'Have you ever had a vain search?' It was safer now, away from herself.

'A couple of times. Both occasions I was with partners in the enterprise. Not that that had anything to do with it—but I prefer to work alone.'

'But if I'm with you, you're not,' she said.

Brent shrugged. 'It's not quite the same thing—I'd already explored, got the feel of the place before you arrived. There's a vast difference which is hard to explain, Donna.'

'And what feelings do you get about the *Maria Grande*?'

He blew smoke out slowly, head partially turned away, face intent on her question. 'There's something there, I'm sure of it. But what—yet—I don't know.'

Emboldened by the rich, sweet liqueur which had a warming, exhilarating effect, Donna said: 'Yet even while you're away like this, still you work?'

'Oh yes,' he answered quietly. 'I can't just leave that. Which, as you will have seen, explains the computer.'

'No, it doesn't! But I won't ask.'

'You wouldn't have hesitated a day or so ago. Is the island exerting its spell on you so quickly?'

'Perhaps.' Donna ran her finger round the rim of the half empty glass; it was faintly sticky.

'And perhaps I'll tell you. I work *with* computers. So you see, in a way I'm just keeping in practice.'

'I see.' But she didn't, and she sensed he was taking pleasure in taunting—no, that was too strong a word— teasing her. She wouldn't give him the satisfaction of seeing she was bothered one way or another. 'May I pour some more coffee?'

'Surely.' His mouth was not twitching with amusement, it *wasn't*. It was just her imagination. But the first time he left the boat, she was going to peep, and she didn't care. So she smiled as he poured her a second cup of coffee, and she said:

'I think I'll go up to the pool and wash my hair.'

'Think you'll find your way?'

'With a torch, yes.' Up there, I can think, can be entirely alone. I have a lot to think about. A great deal. . . .

'Then I shall probably continue work in my study. But not too late—remember our early start in the morning.'

'I'll remember,' she answered.

The pool was cool, refreshing to see after the humidity of the day. She needed no torch once there. The velvet-canopied sky was diamond-sparkled, and a pale moon cast ghostly shadows that silvered the water. It

was a magic place at night, a trysting place for lovers,
but she was alone. Maybe, she thought, I always will
be, even when I'm with others, or in a crowd. Brent
had asked her after dinner if the island was exerting its
spell on her. Perhaps, in a way, it was. It was causing
her to think deeply—or was it Brent himself who was
casting that spell? Her thoughts about him were no
longer clear-cut, but blurred, and that had the power
to disturb. And he had, albeit unwittingly, brought
back memories that had lain hidden in her subconscious mind for nearly eleven years—she didn't know
what he had done or said to trigger them off. She
didn't *want* to know. She wanted them to *go* away.

Taking a deep breath, she stripped off her clothes,
stepped over the rocky edge to the pool, and sank
down into the water, shivering slightly, but for
moments only, at the first cool touch on her bare flesh.
Then—oh, it was bliss! She would concentrate only on
how lovely and *cool* she was and let all other thoughts
go back where they belonged. She shampooed her hair
vigorously and lay back to rinse it off, repeated the
process, then washed herself all over. Standing up, she
stepped out, rubbed herself with the towel and donned
a clean pair of shorts and tee-shirt. Her skin tingled,
her hair was really squeaky clean. She felt *good*.

The journey back down was easier and she reached
the beach, switched off the torch, and looked towards
the boat. Brent was clearly visible in the light flooding
out from his study window, and Donna stood in the
darkness and watched him as, dark head bent, he
spoke into the radio microphone. He wore earphones,
he was apparently reading something out, and he was
totally engrossed in his task. A faint column of smoke
rose from the ashtray, a forgotten cheroot smouldering

away. He worked *with* computers? He had made himself sound like a salesman when he had told her that. No salesman could leave his job and swan off to the Caribbean—and wherever else he had been treasure-seeking—without finding himself very rapidly out of employment. Her curiosity was growing stronger. Almost unaware that she was doing so, Donna remained where she was and watched him, drinking everything in, as absorbed as he, yet not conscious of why she did so. Then, after what seemed like only minutes to her, Brent took off the headphones, touched a switch and turned towards the door. Guiltily aware that if he saw her standing where she was he would be well aware of her visual eavesdropping, Donna, without thinking, darted back into the dark shelter of the trees and stood there, heart thumping, and thinking—why on *earth* am I hiding?

She had moved not a moment too soon. The next second his dark outline blocked the light, huge shadows cast, and he was at the rail. He raised his hands to cup round his mouth, and shouted: 'Donna!' The voice echoed past her, dying away, and she did the only thing possible if she were not to look a complete idiot—she emerged from the trees as if just having arrived, walked towards the boat and answered: 'I'm here.'

Brent looked down; at least he appeared to move his head. The light shining out behind him made it difficult to see him properly. 'Where the *hell* have you been all this time?' he demanded. 'I thought I was going to have to go up to the pool to fetch you!'

Watching you, she answered in her head, then out loud: 'As you can see, that won't be necessary.' Her heart had slowed nearly to normal. Nearly. As he reached over to help her aboard, and her hand was grasped by his, there was the merest thread of something approaching an electric shock at the contact—but that could easily have been static, she thought.

Standing on deck, she looked up at the giant towering over her. He really was *very* big. 'How tall are you?' she asked.

'Good God! You really do make some remarkable *non sequiturs*! Six-five. Where do *you* get your hair cut?'

'What?' Her jaw dropped. What on *earth*?

'Precisely! As *non sequitural* as you—but I'm not supposed to be surprised——'

'There's no such word as *sequitural*,' Donna said crushingly.

He laughed and turned away. 'There is now,' he said, and on that equally crushing exit line, vanished down the companionway. She pulled her tongue out and followed him down. The truce had been brief, fun while it lasted—yet was this battle of wits and wills in a way not even more exhilarating?

'I'm going to bed,' she told his retreating back, 'and thanks for your kind thoughts in coming to the rescue.'

'I didn't need to, did I?' He turned at the galley doorway and looked at her. 'You were just returning, weren't you?' She couldn't quite meet his eyes; he saw too much. 'And dry your hair before you go to bed.'

'It will dry naturally.' They were in the galley now and he flung a towel at her.

'Rub it.'

'Is that an order?' Her mouth set in a mutinous line, Donna stared at him, and thought—My God, he's bossy! No one ever told her what to do—or hadn't until now, with the possible exception of her father, who told everybody what to do all the time and expected to be obeyed. But not this one as well. She wasn't going to have *that*!

'Yes, it is.'

She flung the towel back at him and stalked out, laughing at his sheer effrontery, went into her cabin and slammed the door behind her. If she hadn't done that, it would have been all right. She sat on the bed, picked up her comb and began to comb the thick wet tangled locks. She had switched on the small reading light over her bed and it cast dark shadows where it didn't reach. Then it happened. She had been watching the door, and was just debating whether to bolt it—when the handle turned. And in that simple action, in that frozen, heart-stopping second of time, between Brent actually starting to open the door and actually opening it, all the terrible memories came crowding in in a relentless rush, and would no longer be denied. It had been a door handle turning, a bedroom door *slowly* opening that had started that hidden, never-to-be-told nightmare for her all those long years ago.

She screamed with the force of renewed shock, tried to stand up—but couldn't; nor could she breathe—just as then—then—then——She saw the man coming in again and it was happening almost as if in slow motion—he was there, that man—the same one——

She raised her hands in a gesture of self-defence, across her breasts—the next moment Brent had caught hold of her and was saying something, but his words were a meaningless jumble from a great distance, hidden away from her by the deafening roar of sound from inside her head. He had pulled her to her feet. She was dimly aware of that, of the strength of his hands on her frantically flailing arms, even more dimly aware that it hadn't been like this that other time, but the grey rushing sound was inside her head and her body; like a giant waterfall drowning her, drowning. . . .

A stillness and quiet as of a storm having passed, a certain calm. Donna could open her eyes, and did. And she could move. It was Brent who watched her from the side of the bed, with an inscrutable expression on his face. She was aware of a pungent scent in her nostrils and saw that he held a small bottle. Seeing her eyes open, he said quietly: 'Smelling salts. They won't hurt you.'

She waved them away, but weakly, and he said: 'Hadn't you better tell me what that was all about, in case it happens again?' But he wasn't angry, she could sense that. And it was all right. It had all happened too long ago——

'No, I can't,' she whispered.

'Damn it, *yes!*' Quick anger now, hard swift anger. 'You screamed as though I was going to rape you——'

'No!' She put her hands to her ears to shut out his words and he wrenched them away and held her arms apart so that she was helpless.

'Something happened—to you. It wasn't here, now, on this boat, because there are only the two of us here—so something triggered off a fear in you so great that you screamed out, and when I came near you, you acted as though——' he paused as if to consider his words, continued more quietly: 'You acted as though

you were being threatened by something terrible—and
I want to know what it is.'

'The door handle,' she whispered, and began to
shake, and Brent released her arms and did something
rather surprising. He took hold of her hands instead,
but gently.

'Yes——?'

'It—when you—it moved, when you were about to
come in—it brought back——' Donna's eyes were
filled with tears, and her body was rigid, shaking with
that fine tremor she could not help.

'It brought back a memory of something terrible
that happened when you were younger—a child?'

'I was twelve——' she heard his indrawn breath,
saw his eyes change. 'I was home on holiday from
boarding school. It was summer——' she hesitated. 'I
can't tell you—I've never told a living soul, not even
Nonie.'

'Donna, you can—you must. It had done something
to you, this—thing—whatever it was.'

'Yes—no—I'd forgotten it——'

'Only on the surface. Deep down, it was there,'

'But I can't—I can't——'

Brent did something else equally surprising, he
reached down to her, lifted her so that she was sitting,
and put his arms round her. 'You're safe here, you
know that,' he whispered. 'There's nothing can harm
you.' His voice was soothing. But more that that, his
arms were. They were strong and gentle and cradled
her as though she were a child, and filled her with his
strength, and in so doing, eased her. For long
moments they were silent. The faintest scent of
aftershave drifted into her nostrils, and his hair smelt
of the sea water, and his face was so near, so very

near—but she was safe. She knew that. She took a deep shuddering breath, and his grip tightened, but fractionally.

'It was—late,' she whispered. 'I was at our home in London, and it was late evening, and I'd gone to bed. There was the housekeeper in the house, and one of the maids, that was all.'

'Where were your family?'

Of course, she had to tell him that. That was important too. Everything was becoming clearer; she was *there* now, could recall with a painful clarity everything that had happened on that fateful evening, from early afternoon when she had been to a friend's house and they had had a pleasant schoolgirl gossip about fellow pupils and staff at their boarding school. It had been a fun-filled afternoon, and Dawkins the chauffeur had taken her home at six ready for an early dinner because Mother was going out to the theatre. . . .

'My father was away on business, my two sisters on holiday in Nice, at our house there with several friends. I was too young to go——' she faltered. 'Mother and I were at home alone, and we ate an early dinner because she was going to the theatre with some of her friends. And at nine-thirty I went to bed because I was tired——' She stopped. The memories were too raw and painful. No, not memories; more than that. She felt as she had then, saw her bedroom as it had been, her books and games, in the cupboards, her battered teddy that she refused to throw away— what had happened to that?—the pink velvet curtains drawn back, window open, the heavy net curtains moving in a slight breeze. . . .

She had dozed, she told him, as she relived those last peaceful hours, after drinking the bedtime chocolate that Mrs Dawkins had prepared, and she was awoken by the faint sound of the front door closing, but not sufficiently to want to get up. It would be her mother returning, and she might look in to say goodnight; sometimes she did, sometimes she didn't. . . .

The words came out, more slowly, painfully now, her throat dry with the unshed tears of a twelve-year-old reliving something so awful that she had blanked it out of her mind ever since. 'Then—then—m-my bedroom door was closed, I must have been asleep again since hearing the front door—it was a warm night, and it was very dark outside——' She tried to breathe. It was like that other time now, the air still and warm, and she moved slightly, and Brent, his hands round her back, rubbed her skin with featherlight touch, soothed, comforted. 'And—I heard the door handle being turned, ever so softly, the—it was a brass handle, one of those heavy old-fashioned ones, and the moonlight caught it and I saw it moving—and I thought—it was my m-mother coming in to say goodnight, you see, and I was lying there, thinking, she's remembered—and then—then——' Wide-eyed, she clutched hold of Brent, her body convulsed with the first terrible fear, her fingers digging into his back, gasping for breath. 'No——'

'And it wasn't your mother,' he said.

'It was—a man, a very big man—and he——' she was sobbing now, dry racking sobs as she relived the nightmare—'and I couldn't move—or breathe—I——'

'Ssh—there, relax, take your time——' His face, next to hers, his words whispered, so soft, so soothing, his hands infinitely strong.

'And he came over to the bed—and I—I was too

terrified—he was so big—and I wanted to scream—
and then——' Donna clutched convulsively at him—
'he saw me—and I closed my eyes because I couldn't
look, and I heard him bending over—I smelt whisky
on his breath. Then——' she relaxed slightly—'he
turned and backed away, and he knocked my chair
over—I heard it fall—then I heard the door opening,
closing—and I was alone.'

'Is that it? He didn't touch you?' Brent's voice held
puzzlement. But *he* didn't know the rest.

Donna shook her head. 'No, he never—he never
touched me—but I couldn't move—I thought he
would come back. I wanted my mother, b-but I didn't
know where she was—I——'

'Wait—stay there. You need a drink.'

'No, don't leave me!'

'I'll only be gone a moment, I promise you. You're
safe now.' Donna relaxed her tense hold on him and
he slipped out, to return within ten seconds with a
bottle and glass. He poured her out a small measure.
'Brandy—drink that, it will make you feel better.'

She sipped it, and it did, then handed him the glass.
'Hold me,' she whispered. 'Please—hold me——'

Brent put his arms round her. 'You see——' she
went on, 'that wasn't the worst part. When—after—
when I could move, I was still so frightened, but I
wanted—I wanted my—mother—and I got out of bed,
and I went along—her room is next but one to mine,
you see—and I needed——' she stopped. No, she
mustn't say the rest. That was the worst thing of all.

'I don't think you need to tell me any more, Donna,'
Brent said very quietly.

'But it was so—so awful——' She gulped. 'I still
can't—believe——'

'It's all right. I think I know,' he cut in.

'But you can't *know*——'

'He was with her, wasn't he?' said flatly, voice devoid of inflection. She shuddered. For long endless moments, a waiting silence, then:

'Yes.'

'And that has stayed with you, those memories, ever since?'

'If—you see, it was my fault. I *saw* them—and then—a few days later, my mother left my father—and if I hadn't *seen* them——'

'For God's sake!' he burst out. 'Is *that* what you thought, all these years?'

His outburst shocked her more than she could have imagined, and she began to weep helplessly. How could he understand? If she hadn't gone along to her mother's room and seen—awful things—if she hadn't *seen* it would have all been all right. But she had. 'I—thought he was hurting her,' she choked, through her sobs—'and I screamed and tried to pull him——'

'Dear God,' he whispered, shaken. 'And because of that, you've blamed yourself all this time? He held her firmly away from him and looked deep into her eyes. 'It had *nothing* to do with you, Donna, you must understand that.'

But she closed her eyes and looked down, at the bed, and didn't see the look of terrible compassion and comprehension on his face as he added:

'And you've borne the burden of that for eleven years, because of someone mistaking a bedroom. My *God*—no wonder——'

Donna had scarcely heard. She was so desperately tired, now that at last she had brought such painful events to light, that her brain refused to function any more. But there was relief too, as if in the telling she had exorcised some ghost of the past, a sense of a terrible burden being lifted. That also was exhausting her. . . . 'I want to sleep,' she murmured. 'I'm so very tired——'

'Then you shall. Are you sure you'll be all right if I leave you?'

'Yes, I'm sure.' She was being eased back, to lie down, and she turned her head into the pillow, then Brent pulled up a sheet over her, and she was dimly aware of that too, of feeling protected and cared for, and it was a luxury she had not experienced for too many years—of another *person* caring, caring. . . . And it was thus she drifted into slumber, unaware that he stayed for a while, unaware certainly of his thoughts—which was just as well, for she would have found them disturbing, unaware of anything save colourful dreams that were no longer frightening.

It was the most horrific sound which woke her simultaneously with the violent rocking of the boat. Crash! Something fell with an appalling splintering sound—instantly awake, Donna scrambled out of bed and was immediately sent sprawling against the wall of the cabin as the boat seemed to lift, then fall——

'Brent!' she screamed. 'Brent——' She heard a thunderous roar—not this time in her head, but from a distance, and it was following by another, and another, and jagged lightning flashes filled the cabin in quick succession. She scrambled to her feet, wrenched the crazily banging door open and staggered along the sloping floor of the companionway to Brent's cabin. Another searing, blinding flash of yellow light illuminated it briefly—enough to see that his bed was empty. Her heart contracted in

such terrible fear that she thought she would fall.
The fear was not for herself, it was for him. And as
another horrendous roll of thunder reverberated
round the boat, she knew the final truth about
herself. Knew that she loved him.

CHAPTER SEVEN

'BRENT!' Donna screamed it this time, ran out of his cabin, and along towards the deck. The boat was mercifully still for the time being. How long that would last she had no idea; but if he wasn't aboard the boat he must be on land—and she had to find him. She heard an answering shout. Even as she reached the deck he was clambering aboard, drenched, half naked, but safe. 'Brent——'

'Get below, for God's sake!' He bundled her down the steps, and into the galley, in darkness. It was immediately apparent where the crashes had come from. Cupboards had been wrenched open with the violence of the storm, and crockery and cutlery lay scattered—and shattered—over the floor. Even in the darkness broken shards gleamed whitely. Brent pulled her down on to the bench and held her, his wet body instantly soaking her thin nightdress. She clung to him, uncaring now of anything except the fact that he was safe.

'Where had you——' she began, to be cut off by a deafening, crashing roll of thunder that shook the cabin, followed so immediately by yet another that speech was impossible. Brent had braced his legs against the table which, being fixed, provided an anchor for them, and while the boat rocked, and they with it, at least they were not at the mercy of the elements as everything else had been. He held fast to her, and she to him. Speech of any sort was impossible, but there was touch. To be held by him thus was important, she was safe, so safe. And if they died, it would be together. If—if—— His arms were so strong, wrapped around her; Donna could feel the tension in them spread through from his legs, the tremendous pressure he was exerting on the table, the strength he needed to keep them from being thrown about.

She had started counting in her head now. Impossible before, both lightning and thunder had been almost simultaneous, but now, unbelievably, there was breathing space in between. Just two or three precious seconds at first, then more, then ten or eleven. And for a full half minute—she counted— there was a lull. Both were drenched, both shivering with cold; she wanted to warm him with her love, to make him safe—she wanted—'Brent,' she whispered, 'it's passing.'

'I know.' He took a deep breath. 'Thank God.' They did not move; to do so might have been to tempt fate. Instead they both watched as now, outside, the yellow night turned to black as the flashes grew more intermittent, the thunder more distant, still like a caged wild animal roaring with rage, but less fiercely. And when at last, a full minute elapsed, Brent unpeeled himself from her. 'Stay there—I'm going to get a towel,' he said, and moving cautiously across the debris-covered floor, he reached one and brought it back. Donna was shivering violently with cold and delayed shock, and she whispered:

'I thought you'd gone. I shouted——'

'I'd heard the storm approaching, was worried about your plane, and went over the side to make it secure. I'd only just reached it when the full fury of the storm struck, so I dived into the trees and burrowed into a hollow—when you saw me was the first opportunity I'd had to move——'

'You went out in *this* to see my plane!' she was aghast. 'You could have been killed!'

'That thought did occur to me as I crouched only a few dozen yards from the boat! I had to get back to you, though—I knew you'd have woken by then.' He passed her the towel. 'I could do with a good stiff whisky—if there's any left unbroken.'

'Let me go and see——' He caught her arm.

'Watch your feet. Don't tread on any broken pots.'

'I won't,' she assured him. 'I'll go——'

'I'm going to get dry clothes on.' He stood up to follow her. The boat lay at an odd angle, but it wasn't listing as much as it had at one point. It was too early—and too dark—to assess the extent of any major damage, but they could move easily, and the structure of the vessel was solid. Donna crossed her fingers superstitiously as she went into the main lounge, felt her way across to the drinks cupboard and, pulling a face at what she might find, opened it. All the bottles and glasses were fitted into wooden layers with holes in, and this was what had saved them from the fate that had befallen the crockery. Laughing in sheer relief, she lifted a bottle of whisky out very carefully, and a tumbler, then made her cautious way out to his cabin. Brent was in bed, and a candle in a holder burned at the side of him. Donna was about to put the bottle down when she saw the blood, and for a moment, her heart stood still. In the flickering gleam of the candle, she could see the dark shadow of welling blood on Brent's forehead near his left temple. And he was unaware of it, that was obvious. Very slowly she put the bottle and glass down. 'Brent,' she said, 'don't you know you've cut your head?'

He reached up, touched, looked at his hand, sticky with blood. 'Lord,' he said. 'I must have started it off again when I rubbed myself with that towel.' He looked at her. 'It seems worse than it is,' he told her. 'I got a crack on the head as I left the trees to come back here—a branch, but I thought it was okay.'

Donna poured out some whisky, hand steady, strangely in complete control now. 'Where's your first aid box?' she asked evenly.

'In the galley, cupboard beneath the bench where we sat. Watch your feet.'

'I will. Drink that.'

She was back a minute or so later. The candlelight was not too bright, but sufficient to see what she was doing. Her fear, that Brent might have concussion, seemed to be unfounded, and the wound seemed to worry him far less than it did Donna herself. She cleaned the cut—a deep gash—with antiseptic, and bandaged it firmly. Delayed reaction hit her when it was done, and she sat down, legs very shaky, and took a good swallow of his whisky. Distant rumblings and even more distant flashes of lightning were the only sounds now, apart from the ceaseless rain which drummed on the windows and sides in a relentless, non-stop staccato.

Brent eased himself away slightly, to make room, and opened the covers of his bed. 'Lie down, Donna,' he said. 'You look more shattered than I feel,' and she, because it was the most natural thing in the world, crawled into bed beside him and put her arms around him. He was warmer now, and so was she. She gave a long sigh.

'I never want to live through anything like that again,' she said, her voice muffled against his chest.

He was absentmindedly stroking her shoulders. '*That* was a twenty-four-carat, one-in-a-million zinger of a storm,' he murmured. 'I've been around and I've never experienced anything like that before, and hope to God I never will again. But we made it, didn't we?' His breath was warm against her cheek. There was, so strangely, and she didn't pause to think why, nothing remotely sexual in his embrace. It was as if two people who have been through something terrible were clinging together afterwards in sheer thankfulness and relief at having survived. No more than that. She *needed* to be with him, she knew that. And perhaps, at that moment he needed her.

He had put a blanket over his sheet. It was necessary, because the storm had left the air cooler, damp. The first faint fingers of the dawn light crept into the room as the candle gutted and died, and all was quiet outside as the rain, unknown to them, pattered to a halt. For both slept, locked in each other's arms, as deeply asleep—and perhaps as innocent—as two children.

It was a shaft of sunlight that woke Donna first, slanting on her cheek, warm and bright. She opened her eyes, puzzled, then remembered where she was. It had been a deep sleep, untroubled by dreams, only vaguely pleasant memories fading as fast as thought. Then she turned her head to see Brent asleep beside her, the bandage across his forehead showing white in contrast to his tan. There was only a faint smear of blood on it. That he was deeply asleep was evidenced by the fact that even when she moved, he did not stir. Donna, who by now was wide awake, slipped very carefully out of bed and crept along to the galley to assess the extent of the damage. Her first impression was that a bomb had hit it. Cupboards lay open, their contents spilled out—tinned food, cups, plates, knives and forks all scattered on the floor, but as she looked around more carefully, she could see that it was superficial damage. The refrigerator door had remained locked, the stove seemed not to have been touched. She lit the gas, filled the kettle, and after putting it on to heat, walked quietly up on deck. There was devastation all around; trees uprooted, branches strewn over the beach, but worst of all—the boat was jammed against the rocks. She peered over the side, fearful, then scrambled down, waded to look, was stunned by the sight that met her eyes.

The side directly below Brent's study window was bowed in with the giant rock that crushed mercilessly against it. It explained the list to the boat—but miraculously, it seemed, the side, though buckled, had not been pierced. Donna looked round to where she had left her plane, and at first didn't believe her eyes. A huge tree had crashed on to it, and was wedged between the floats. And he had gone to check it! If he hadn't returned when he had, he would surely have been killed, or at the very least, badly injured. Sickness rose in Donna, making her feel dizzy with the realisation. He could have died—and she would never have even known, until now, because it would have been impossible to see. Shaken beyond words, she scrambled aboard, walked dazedly into the galley and made herself a cup of strong black coffee. And if he had died, she thought, I would not have wanted to go on living. Life would have held no meaning for her ever again. She began to shiver uncontrollably, the cup shaking so much in her hands that she had to put it down. She saw the pattern of her life unfolding before her; and it had all been leading up to this moment, when she had realised at last what it meant to love someone more than herself.

She stared blindly towards the window and the scene of devastation outside. It had taken a storm to show her the truth. Without that she might never have known the wrenching ache of loss. Without that—and the other, no less devastating storm of before, when she had at last been able to tell what she had hidden even from herself for so many years—she would not have been made aware of something so blindingly obvious that her only surprise now was that it had taken so long.

I love him. The words, said inside her head, were a kind of music that only she could hear. She put her half empty cup down, and tiptoeing carefully over the dangerous floor, went into Brent's cabin where he lay so fast asleep, and crept into bed beside him and put her arms around him. She wanted—she *needed*—to hold him before he woke, before the precious time was past and gone for ever. He would never love her, for how could she deserve something so rich and precious in return? But at least, here, for a little while longer, she would have something to remember when he was long gone from her life. He stirred, murmured something in his sleep, and she murmured: 'Ssh——'

His body was so warm. Relaxed in sleep he was a different man, his shaggy hair unkempt, his mouth softer and gentler, as if he dreamed pleasant dreams. Their bodies touched and Donna drew strength and something wonderful beyond words from his. She could stay here for ever, and let the world go away.

She put out her hand to stroke his cheek because the urge was overwhelming, and he stirred. Frightened lest he wake now, and spoil the precious few moments they would have, she became very still—and he too. Eyes shining with her love, she watched him, drinking in his features like heady wine, the dark-lashed sleeping eyes, straight nose, darkened jaw, that cleft in his chin, darker still, the smooth hard line of his cheek. His ears—he has lovely ears, she thought, and I never noticed!

Soon she would have to wake him and tell him of the damage she had seen. In a way, it seemed, the storm had been an inevitable climax to a day of ever-mounting tension, building up slowly from a perfect trip to La Barra, which had ended in a lovely dinner—and yet already there had been signs, even then; he had seemed different—and she herself had felt edgy, without knowing why. She knew why, now. All the time, lurking deep in her subconscious mind, had been the fear of a very large man—as Brent undoubtedly was—that had culminated in that explosive scene in her cabin, when his turning of the door handle—such a simple act—had triggered off in her those terrifying moments when she had been a child of twelve. No one had ever been told before, not even Nonie. Donna had locked the deeply shameful incident away, never to be remembered—as she had thought—again.

She went back in time again, here safe now, and recalled those days shortly after that when her mother had left home for the last time. Her parents' divorce had been a stormy one, filled all the papers for weeks at the time. Only she, Donna, had nursed a dreadful knowledge that it had all been her fault. It had made her ill and for several days, at the height of the scandal, she had been in bed tended by the doctor, with a nurse in residence. Her father had had no time to see her, or very little. When he did he was distrait, almost terrifyingly distant, and she thought that perhaps he guessed her part in it—that had been nearly as bad as everything else put together, for how could he love her when *she* was responsible? Even now there was a bitter taste in her mouth as she remembered his face. . . .

She and her sisters had stayed with him, and for a while they had been close, the three girls, united in their common sorrow. Then, all had subtly changed. They were several years older than Donna, Vanessa seventeen at the time it had happened, Amanda nearly twenty, already adults with lives of their own. They had recovered. Or had they? Now, in the light of her new-found awareness, Donna wondered. Had any of them ever got over it? Her mouth twisted in bitterness as she pondered that unanswerable question. She had a recently new stepmother, a woman whom her father had known for many years. Donna avoided her as much as possible, as did her sisters. She had her own flat in London, and visited her father once a fortnight when she was there, but even from a distance he sought to control her life. She supposed he always would. She moved slightly, anguished. There was something she had not told Brent that last night. Something she had been unable to, even then, when he had wrested her story from her, word by painful word, something that was still unbearable, even now. Two years after the divorce, her mother had been killed with her lover while flying in a private plane from Acapulco to Barbados on her way to visit Nonie. Donna shivered helplessly as she at last allowed herself to remember that final, dreadful fact. . . . And that, more than anything, had haunted her ever since.

It was no use; the mood of warmth and love she had felt, the one that had made her seek a brief shelter in Brent's arms, was gone. Very slowly, carefully, she eased herself from his bed and warmth, and, with one last look at his sleeping form, went quietly out of the cabin.

There was work to be done. She, Donna, was a survivor. The Webster clan were winners, always had been, she had to remember that. She was not a helpless female, seeking warmth in any man's arms. For she had seen what happened as a result of that. . . .

She surveyed the galley, eyes dry but bright, the lump of pain in her heart being dissolved with each minute that passed. She had thought she loved him— and there was no such thing, she knew that only too well. She sniffed, took a deep breath, and set to work on clearing the debris and restoring the galley to its original order. Her cup of black coffee, now lukewarm, was a reminder to her of something she preferred to forget.

She was on her knees wiping the cleared floor with a damp soapy cloth when Brent came in. 'Good grief, where's my camera?' he asked, and she looked up smartly. It was all right now, normality was restored. How near she had been to making a complete fool of herself he would never know.

'Someone has to do the work around here,' she retorted, 'and I didn't want to disturb your beauty sleep, Captain!'

'And well you might not. I haven't seen the damage outside yet,' he said. 'I might need all my strength for that.'

'It's not good. We're against a rock—but there's no sign of a hole in the side——'

'Or we'd have known much sooner,' he cut in drily. 'Okay, make me a small coffee will you while I go and see—then we'll dive.'

'Dive!' She stared at him in astonishment and rose slowly to her feet. 'This *morning*? After all——' she gestured round helplessly—'this?'

'Even more so, after "all this",' he responded. 'Don't you see, Donna? If the sea was rough enough to move the boat it could well have shifted the *Maria Grande*. Oh yes, we're diving all right, and as soon as possible.'

For a few moments she regarded him, her thoughts very mixed. Then she nodded. 'I'll make you that coffee.'

'Thanks.' He loped out silently and she put the kettle on. I don't know him at all, she thought. I would have expected him to be half out of his mind with worry about the storm damage—instead of which he's going diving! It gave her a new insight into the character of the decidedly puzzling, complex man with whom she was briefly sharing her life. He would let nothing stand in the way of his purpose—which was, at the moment, to find gold aboard a wrecked Spanish vessel. No wonder he wouldn't let me go when he first met me, she realised; for sheer dedication to a task, he would match Daddy any day. That thought had a sobering effect. To allow herself to fall in love with a man like Brent would be foolish indeed. It would not happen.

The coffee was on the table when he returned. One look at his face was enough to tell her that something was very wrong. 'What is it?' she asked. 'The boat?' Had she mistaken the extent of the damage?

'No, that can be fixed. It's your plane, Donna——'

'I know—a tree fell—but it's——'

'It's unflyable without major repairs, and no way I can do them here,' said Brent, sitting down at the table.

'Then how do I get away?'

He smiled slightly. 'Well, I'm not going to sail off and leave you stranded here, you idiot. We'll have to tow it, won't we?'

'But I have to get it to Barbados!'

'So?' He eyed her coolly over the flame of his lighter. 'It will mean a delay in my journey—a couple of days longer, that's all.'

'Oh!' She digested that, and sat down opposite him, her feelings mixed, most strangely. One part of her wanted to get away—for he knew too much, had seen too much of what was hidden deep inside her, and it was disconcerting, but another part of her felt oddly pleased. An uncomfortable blend of things inexplicable.

'Oh? Lost for words? No point in worrying about it. There's no alternative—unless you have a better suggestion?' Brent tapped cigar ash into the unbroken ashtray she had rescued, and his eyes were strangely expressive.

'No. I just didn't want to put you to any—inconvenience,' she began, to be interrupted by his flat level tones.

'The minute you landed was too late for that.'

'I didn't know *you* were here or I wouldn't bloody well *have* landed!' she shot back, and he raised one eyebrow, mocking, *knowing*.

'Temper! Remember what I told you about that.'

Donna caught her breath. She remembered more,

swallowed back the reply which would have come only too easily days before, and said instead: 'Sorry.' It wasn't easy, in fact it was extremely difficult, just that one word. But something had changed, even though he wasn't to know that.

He nodded. 'What we have to do is accept what has happened—no point in doing otherwise—and proceed from there. Your plane is damaged, *ergo*, you can't fly it. My boat isn't—or not badly—therefore we use that. However, we don't know how long it will be before my task here is completed, and so, like I said, we go diving this morning, take photos, see if anything has shifted down below—and plan accordingly.'

'What about food?' she asked quietly.

'There's more than enough for several weeks. There are also, in case you hadn't noticed, abundant fish in the sea, fruit on the trees, and a never-ending source of water. If we were shipwrecked here for a year, we'd not starve.'

His voice held a flat realism; she knew the truth of his words. She was strangely impressed by them. 'Wouldn't you mind?' she asked, and thought as soon as the words came out—what a ridiculous question!

'Mind?' He seemed to be turning the thought over, then he shrugged. 'Of course I'd mind, but like you, I'm a survivor——' had he read her thoughts?—'and I'd make the most of that year. I'd write the book I've never had time for—I'd jog round the island every evening to keep fit, I'd ration out my precious store of cheroots and drinks to one a week—and I'd probably come off the island after a year a wiser man than when I went on. Does that answer your hypothetical question?'

Donna had to smile. 'Yes, it does.'

'And you? Would you cope?'

'Entirely alone—or with somebody?'

'Either—take your pick?'

'I—would find it very lonely if I were alone, but yes, like you, I'd manage.'

'And—with somebody?'

'I suppose it all depends who that somebody is,' she answered.

'Oh, indeed it does,' Brent agreed gravely, but the spark of mockery that touched his eyes was not imagined, and she felt herself colour.

'There are a great many people I'd prefer not to be with, and in which case I'd rather be on my own.' She hadn't intended the words to come out like that, but they had.

There was a stillness, a waiting for a few endless moments, then he said: 'How true, Donna.'

She couldn't sit there any longer. He had touched a nerve, and she didn't want him to look at her with that all-knowing expression again. 'If you'll excuse me, I'll go and change——'

But he caught her arm as she went past, stopped her, just like that. 'And am I one of those?' he asked softly.

She looked down at his hand on her arm, then slowly raised her eyes to his. They held a disconcerting expression. 'I—don't know *you*, do I?' she said slowly. 'So the answer to that is—I don't *know*.'

Brent released his hold. 'A—sensible answer. No, you don't know me. As I don't really know you.' She could not ask, would not ask, the next, almost inevitable question. For she dreaded his answer.

'Excuse me,' she said, and went out, into her cabin. What would he have answered if she had asked? That he would infinitely prefer being alone to sharing his island with her? Of course he would!

She went and took her suit out of its bag and laid it on the bed. For the first time in her life she had met a man who didn't give a damn about her money, who wasn't impressed by her looks—who saw beneath the surface as no one else ever had. Frightening in a way—yet chastening. For what *did* he see? She looked across at the mirror, saw her reflection, but it told her nothing, only that she had a beautiful face, and the image seemed to mock her hollowly. You are nothing inside, it seemed to say, and he knows it. Knows it, knows it. . . .

She turned away, unable to bear her image any more, then very slowly sank on to the bed. Putting her face in her hands to shut out the world, she felt the welcome release of hot tears. 'Who am I?' she whispered, and the answer came: No one. You are no one. Her body shook.

'Donna? Are you ready?' Brent's voice came from outside her door. She wiped her cheeks and stood up guiltily.

'I won't be a moment——' She fled into her shower cubicle and rinsed her face in cool salty water. Hastily, no time now for introspection, she donned the tight-fitting garment, hopping on one leg as she tried desperately to fit it on. 'Damn, damn,' she muttered. She should have stayed at Nonie's. She would have been all right there. She should never have come here, and then all secrets would have remained safely buried, and it would have been *all right*. . . .

'I'm ready!' she called, and heard his footsteps recede. She took a deep breath. She was going to do everything he told her, exactly as and when he did so.

Head held high, she marched out and up on to the deck, where he waited, watching her.

'Perfect fit, I see,' he remarked as he turned to clamber over the side.

'Yes, isn't it?' She smiled. 'Who knows, we might do better today.'

Brent nodded. He checked the dinghy and they scrambled in. The next minute they were heading for open sea. The air was fresh and sweet, the sea calm, and Donna forced herself to relax. She wasn't going to let him down. This morning she was going to surprise him with her quiet acceptance, her amenability. She had to. She was going to change—and it would all be due to him, only he would never know that. Never. . . .

They had been beneath the water for just over an hour, in that strange and wonderful other world that so few know, and this time it was different. For one thing, they worked as a perfect team. Donna, attuned to his every move, co-ordinated her own to match his, swam down in perfect unison, followed a few feet behind when they reached the wreck, felt herself in some odd way to be a part of him and his search. She wanted him to succeed in his quest; she hadn't much minded before, one way or the other. She had seen him only as an eccentric treasure-seeker on what seemed to her a crazy wild-goose chase beneath the sea. Yet now his excitement gripped her. He was a man like no other she had ever known. The only reason he would fail would be if there were no gold aboard the *Maria Grande*. If there was any—he would find it. And at that moment, as she followed him through barnacle encrusted doorways to reach the hidden heart of the dead ship, there was only that one thought in her mind. All else, the storm, her plane, her own very secret and private distress, all were gone as though they had never been. This was the only world that existed. This—and them, moving ever slower as progress became difficult, both needing all their strength to lift and cast aside huge wooden beams that had been dislodged by the violence of that previous night's storm. For Brent's instincts had been right. The *Maria Grande* had shifted, and lay at an entirely different angle—and deeper, in a hollow on the sea bed—from where it had been before. It was almost as though it had been turned upside down. And in so doing, it had become even more of a wreck—but more accessible.

Donna held his camera and spare torch. He had photographed it as they had made their way in, each dazzling flash illuminating everything in sharp relief, startling the fishes that followed them everywhere—and reminding Donna briefly of the lightning during the storm.

He reached down. Her torch beam had showed the dull gleam—only for an instant—of something metallic. It was the ring of a trapdoor, green with verdigris, but some had been scraped off by the broken spar of wood which had—probably as a result of its shifting during the storm—been jammed against it. Only a fraction of a millimetre, but enough for Donna's sharp eyes to see. Brent tried to lift the ring, then, bending, began to scrape it with his knife. Donna held the torch very steadily on it, watching, her own excitement growing as he did so, each move of his skilled and patient. And she knew suddenly the lure of the search, knew why he had chosen this hobby of his. There *was* excitement in it; it was not madness—or it if was then she too had become part of the madness. What did it matter if there were nothing there after all? The hunt was the important thing, the eternal seeking for that which is hidden from man by nature.

This man would have stories to tell his grand-children that would fire them with the enthusiasm he had known. And I am a part of it, she thought. A small part, but I have been *here*, I have watched, and known his thoughts. I have shared in an adventure containing wonder, beyond the normal, and I shall never forget this moment as long as I live.

Brent's head was bent, his task finished, the ring gleamed a dull gold by his hand. He began to scrape away at the surroundings of it, never glancing up, needing no encouragement. He knew what he was doing, that was the only thing that mattered to Brent. Donna knew now why he had come alone. If he had lived a hundred—two hundred—years ago, he would have been an explorer in the darkest forests of the unknown tropics. Living now, in a world where man had walked on the moon, he had chosen the great unknown beneath the sea, and he was as happy here as anywhere. She felt envy, for someone who had decided what he wanted to do and then gone ahead and done it. He might not even appreciate how rare a man he was—he probably didn't care—there was something magnificent about him, magnificent—and extraordinary.

He turned, signalled her to kneel beside him, pointed. She could see the fine line revealed after his careful knife-work, the rectangular shape of the exposed trapdoor. But where, she wondered, heart beating fast, did it lead to?

In a minute they would find out. . . .

CHAPTER EIGHT

IT was over, or nearly. Someone, perhaps fifty or even a hundred years ago, had been before them, had explored the depths as they had, and had found treasure. It was impossible to know when, but the evidence was there—huge chests wrenched open and left to rot in that sea, now seaweed and barnacle-filled. Except for one small box, no larger than a writing case, that had been left unnoticed, wedged tightly in a corner and visible only after a searching torch probe. Donna would not have seen it, but Brent did, and spent several minutes of extremely careful tapping with a small pointed instrument to loosen it from its niche. He placed it in a net bag which clipped to his belt, then indicated to her that it was time to go up.

No journey had ever been so long. Donna, in a fever of impatience, yet mindful of his strict instructions, obeyed him scrupulously. The box was heavy and impeded his steps back along the tortuous route they had gone into the very bowels of the ship. He led, she followed, their two torch beams lighting an eerie path full of shadows and strange drifting creatures of the underwater world. All became imprinted in her mind, every step, the dark shadowy blur that was Brent, the drift of seaweed that briefly halted their way, like a curtain over a door, to be pushed aside and hacked at, a dark green dangerous curtain that could entrap and smother by its density. Donna was as vividly aware of that as she was of everything else; an added dimension in time and space.

There was no sensation of minutes passing down there, only the now, the every step, and at last, the slow tortuous ascent. Here Brent took her hand, and guided her. It saved signalling, it was an essential part of their journey. The oxygen bubbles rose, small glinting flashes in a gradually lessening gloom, each breath controlled and shallow, each upward yard measured as precisely as though he carried an altimeter. It took nearly as long for them to reach the surface as their entire exploration of the boat, and Donna was exhausted. As she looked up and saw the surface, like a green sky that grew lighter with each passing minute, she knew that she had nearly reached the limit of her physical strength. Brent's hand was as strong and steady as a rock. He was not tired, or gave no evidence of it. And when, for a moment, she faltered in their steady upward pacing, his strength halted her, let her pause to gain equilibrium. His control was absolute.

Now the light was blinding, after that primitive never-ending darkness—a vast green canopy above their heads. Donna had the illusion for a few moments of flying through space, to the outer limits of the universe—and then—a rushing, roaring sound, and they broke the surface. She looked around her, momentarily dazed and disorientated. The dinghy was several dozen yards away, bobbing in a calm sea, Brent's boat *Searcher II* way beyond that, nestling against the shelter of land. A gull perched on the radio mast, then with a cry flew away, soaring upwards, protesting their intrusion.

She had no strength left to scramble aboard the

dinghy, and Brent hauled her up and over the side, where she collapsed, unbuckling her oxygen tank with shaking hands that refused to work properly. He looked down at the box lying beside her and grinned. 'We did it,' he said.

'I can't believe——' she began, and had to stop for breath.

'Don't talk—we were down there quite a time. We'll get aboard, have some food and get changed—then we'll see about opening this little beauty.'

'Someone else had been there,' she managed to say, and he shrugged.

'That's life.' He didn't sound disappointed. Donna knew why, now. She wouldn't have done a week ago, but perhaps she was learning something. He helped her aboard his boat, then went back for the precious box and tools. Donna, holding tightly to the rails, tottered down the companionway into her cabin, and, too exhausted to do anything else, flopped on to her bed. She heard him moving above, then his footsteps passing her cabin, into the galley. The sounds receded, drifted; she closed her eyes and yawned hugely, then fell asleep.

When she awoke she sat up in alarm. She had dreamed of him opening the box without her. . . . 'Brent!' she called, and heard his answering shout.

'Relax. I've been working. It's still intact,' as if he had sensed the note of dismay in her voice. She smiled reluctantly. He was too shrewd by far. However briefly she had dozed, it had refreshed her. Peeling off the by now roasting hot wet-suit, she stripped and showered, looked at the new chiffon dress still in its bag on the floor, thought—why not?—and put it on. She glanced at herself in the mirror. It was a simple design with thin shoulder-straps, then dropping, straight but full so that if she twisted quickly, the skirt swirled around her. The colour was flattering, and very strangely, although it had been a cheap dress, she felt good in it, far better than in many of her more expensive—and exclusive—creations. She didn't think to question it, it just was. She found a pair of thin flat sandals—no one would dare wear heels on board a boat—and went out to find Brent.

He looked up as she entered the galley. For just a moment his eyes lingered, as if in surprise, then he remarked: 'I thought the smell of food would wake you,' and she saw the pan simmering on the cooker, the kettle with steam rising from it, and she laughed.

'It didn't. I dreamt you'd opened the box——'

'You make me feel like a quizmaster,' he observed. 'What's the dress for? A celebration? There might be nothing to celebrate.'

'True.' She sat down, smoothing the skirt demurely round her.

'Would you mind? If it was empty, I mean?'

'For your sake, perhaps, but,' she shrugged, 'the adventure alone was worth it.'

Brent had his back to her, attending to whatever cooked in that pan. At her reply he turned to look at her, his mouth curving slightly as if in amusement. 'Well, well,' he said.

'Meaning?' She raised her eyebrows.

'Merely an observation.'

'Meaning—good gracious, there's a change!' she responded swiftly.

'Something like that.'

'There is.'

'What? A change?' He paused, set out two plates,

and added: 'It wouldn't be you, without the fire.' His voice was dry. He spooned out what looked like scrambled eggs and put the plates on the table. He had already buttered bread, and put salt and pepper beside that plate. Then he sat down. Donna hadn't replied. His words had taken her aback, both the words themselves and the tone in which they were said. 'Eat,' he added in almost kindly tones, 'before it gets cold.'

It wouldn't be you, without the fire. Strange thing to say. How odd too, the effect on Donna. She cleared her throat. 'Um—did you have a doze as well?'

'Nope. I had a few things to check, and I did. There's no major damage anywhere—except to your plane. I hope it's insured.'

'It is. Is your computer all right?'

'Bloody but unbowed.'

'Talking of which, how's your head?' He sported a large plaster instead of the bandage, she had noticed that the moment she had walked into the galley.

'Ditto there. I'll live.'

'You were very lucky you didn't get worse than that,' she remarked. 'These eggs are delicious—I was starving!'

'So was I. Don't tell me you'd have been worried?'

'About your being hungry? Not particularly.' She smiled inwardly at her flippancy.

'Smart question! You know damned well I didn't mean that.'

'Oh! About you being injured? Well, I suppose I would have *had* to look after you, wouldn't I?'

'Spoken like a true Webster,' he said softly—and it wasn't funny any more. She looked down at her plate, and the swift cutting retort died unspoken. His rapier thrust, perhaps not even intended, had pierced to her heart. She took a deep breath and pushed the plate, eggs half eaten, away.

'Excuse me,' she said. 'I——' she couldn't speak. She went quickly out, into her cabin, and leaned against the door. Brent made no move to follow her. She heard no steps, no voice calling her. She heard only the sound of crockery, a knife and fork moving, then silence. Donna breathed deeply and slowly, calming herself. The simplicity of his words, and the devastating effect they had had, still stunned her. Five words: Spoken like a true Webster—which summed up everything about herself and all those nearest to her in one incisive thrust. Wide-eyed, dry-eyed, she stared round her, seeing with sharply awakened eyes the bitter reality of her existence. He hadn't meant to wound her so deeply, but he had, and more effectively than she could ever have imagined. It must not show. That was vital to her very being. She must go back now. *Now*. Taking a deep breath, she wrenched open the door and returned steady-footed, carefully, into the galley.

'Something in my eye,' she told him, even managing to smile. She rubbed her left eye to lend credence to her words, and sat down again. The meal resumed. They even conversed, Brent telling her that he would be moving the boat after they had eaten to enable him to see what repairs, if any, the side would need, Donna nodding, agreeing in all the right places, listening intently. But it wasn't the same. Things had changed, a slight shifting of balance, a heightened awareness. And he didn't smile—not once. His eyes, when he spoke, had a dark shuttered look, as if his feelings and thoughts were not for her to know.

It was a relief to be finished eating, to clear the pots,

to wash them, open the window and throw out the scraps for the attendant gulls. The box waited to be opened, but something there had changed too. No longer that delicious sense of anticipation that had enhanced their return. It didn't matter. She would watch him open it, she would exclaim as if pleased if there were anything of historic or intrinsic value, she would not let him down. But the magic was destroyed, and he would never know why, for her, it had gone.

A true Webster—true Webster—remnants of an echo remained. The meaning went beyond the mere words had. Websters were special people, rich, secure in that wealth—and arrantly selfish beyond anything. She had known it, had always known it, all her life. Websters took what they wanted and never stopped to consider the price. Her father, her sisters, aunts, uncles, cousins, all a part of the giant Webster clan of winners—*wherever they went*. Brent had, by that simple, devilishly simple remark, shown her something that no one had ever done before, as though he had held a mirror of truth up to her, and in it she had seen what the whole world, outside their charmed circle, had always known but never dared say.

Yet had he not shown her compassion when she had been distressed? He had held her like the child she had temporarily become, and brought her out of the depths of despairing memory. He could be cruel, sharp and incisive with words and looks—he also possessed the gentleness that is the greatest mark of true strength. For a few hours, she thought, I knew what it would be like to be loved by him. But no more, no more. He would never see that other vulnerable side of her again. She dared not let him see.

The boat rocked, she heard footsteps; he was

returning. Bright-faced, calm-eyed, Donna turned as he entered the galley. 'Everything all right?'

'Yes. It's just as well I have to return to Barbados with you, though. I'll get it into a boatyard and let them look at it.' He ran his fingers through his thick wet hair—he had been in the sea, because he was drenched, dripping water with every step. He took the towel, gave himself a perfunctory rub down and said: 'It's time, I think.'

'Yes.' She looked across at the box on a working surface and watched him carry it over and set it down on several sheets of newspaper on the table. The box was about sixteen inches across, a foot deep, about the same from front to back. Thickly encrusted with shellfish and tangled seaweed, it was difficult to tell whether the original surface had been polished or carved. There was no apparent opening either. He laid out several tools beside it; a lethal-looking knife, a chisel and a hammer. For a few minutes he studied it, turning it round, even upside down, then on its edge. The box was giving no secrets away. Squat and silent, it stood on the table looking as though it would be impervious to everything.

He began tapping with the chisel, feeling the crusted surface for the line between lid and bottom. 'Hold it, will you?' he said, face intent. Donna obeyed, felt the vibrations with each blow struck, but keeping a tight grip, legs braced under the table as if that would help. An hour later, the last remaining shells and debris were removed and what remained was an old carved wooden box, its surface pitted with the salt water, but clearly showing a design of flowers curving gracefully round lid and sides. There was a brass keyhole in it, green with verdigris. Donna wondered where the key was now, if it had perished, still worn round some Spanish *doña*'s neck on a black ribbon. It brought a poignant sense of immediacy from the distant past. Someone had locked that box for the last time, and now, two hundred years later, it was to be opened, whatever had been so carefully placed inside it still there. Brent gave the lock a swift sure blow. Chisel placed just so, hammer poised, and—crack! It was done. Donna, despite her unhappiness, felt an irresistible lift of her heart. He looked up. 'Want to open it?' he asked.

She smiled, shook her head. 'This one is definitely yours.'

He held the base of the box with one hand, and with the other prised the lid slowly upwards. She glanced quickly at him as he did so. What thoughts were going through his head at this moment? Did he feel a sense of great triumph? He couldn't be entirely unmoved, even although his face was giving away as little as the box had. He was expressionless, concentrating to the exclusion of all else on what he was doing. And the task of lifting the lid took up much strength.

Then—and oh, then, there it was! A bundle of fragile-looking material, possibly silk, and very yellowing, was revealed. Carefully Brent reached in and lifted it out. It was heavy, and fragments of cloth dissolved like gossamer in the sunlight even as he took it up. He laid the bundle down on the table, and Donna leaned forward, she couldn't help it, holding her breath. He peeled back the crumbling threads— and there, nestling at the very heart of it all, was a jumbled collection of dull gold jewellery, caught in the sunlight, its first in two centuries. There were rings and chains, pendants and bracelets, some heavy, some as fine as threads themselves.

'Oh—how utterly beautiful! May I?'

'Feel free.' He picked up a heavy gold ring with a huge garnet winking ruby-red as he held it to the light, and Donna lifted out a bracelet that was so exquisite in design that tears came to her eyes. Someone had once worn this, had admired it, held it up to the light, as she was doing. . . . It was like golden lace, fine filigree caught with tiny sapphires in heart-shaped motif round it, hundreds of sapphires in all. She laid it over her wrist and looked at it, moved far beyond anything she had imagined she would be. This was living history.

She put the bracelet down on the paper and lifted a fine chain on which hung a teardrop-shaped diamond. Dulled with years of immersion, nevertheless the diamond still held a sparkling glint of fire in its depths. Donna possessed jewellery, some exquisite pieces handed down through the family, and to her they were a part of her life—she had never really *looked* at anything properly, or thought of the history, merely worn whatever bauble she chose when the occasion demanded. There was something humbling in thus seeing this small collection, an appreciation of fine craftsmanship.

'Try that on, it might fit.' Brent handed her the ring, which was surprisingly heavy—and small. Her little finger was the only one it would fit on. She held her hand up to admire it and for a moment it seemed as though a ghostly hand reached out to touch hers; imagination of course, but. . . .

'Mmm. What can I say?' she whispered. 'It—it——'

'Fair takes your breath away?' he suggested, and she looked up.

'Something like that,' she agreed. She had to tell

him—now. 'I didn't really understand your desire to explore the depths before,' she said quietly. 'I do now.' She paused. 'These shouldn't lie buried at the bottom of the ocean. They deserve to be—seen.'

'And worn.' He was moving the box, lifting from a drawer a rolled-up piece of dark blue material which he spread out over the newspaper. Then he laid all the separate pieces on the blue velvet and picked up his camera. Donna took the ring off her finger and laid it down with its fellows.

'For the record?' she asked, her tone light.

'Yes.' He was aiming the camera, focussing it, and she turned away when the flash came. He took several photographs, moving round slightly after each, while Donna waited. Then it was done. He rolled up the jewellery in the cloth and said: 'I'm going to put these in the safe,' and went out. Of course, he would have a safe, she thought. She wondered what else he had in it. She brushed the shells and drying seaweed from the table, put them in the waste bin, and wiped the table down.

That was it. All over. Treasure found, mission accomplished, and time to leave the island. And soon, perhaps tomorrow, it would be goodbye. She would go to Nonie's. And Brent? After having his boat repaired, he would set off for England—or somewhere else. Perhaps he had further maps in his safe of more treasure spots. He certainly wouldn't tell Donna. She remembered his blazing anger when she had arrived, as if she might be a spy. And she had thought *he* was a criminal on the run! Which only goes to show, she thought, how wrong we can be about people we meet. How very wrong. . . .

In a few weeks she would return to London. Brent

hadn't once asked her where she lived. Why should he? She was a true Webster—she blinked back a tear. He would imagine her—if indeed he thought of her at all—resuming the mad social whirl. There was no way she could or would tell him that all that had been irrevocably changed, in just a few brief bitter-sweet days. She didn't know yet what she was going to do, but she knew what she had finished with, and for ever.

She needed a swim. She needed the cool touch of clean salt water to cleanse her spirit. She was weary and heartsick with a pain that refused to go away. She went into her cabin, bolted the door, stripped her new dress off and changed into her black swimsuit. She could hear, as she passed Brent's study, the sound of a typewriter. 'I'm going for a swim!' she called.

A pause in the tapping. 'Right,' he called back, and the sounds resumed. Donna had the awful empty feeling that, now it was all over, he had put her out of his mind, and if her plane, and his boat, hadn't been damaged, he would have told her he was leaving. She climbed over, down the steps, and struck away from the boat, swimming strongly, the water silken smooth against her skin, making her feel better physically. Only the inner anguish remained, and that would take a long time to fade, and perhaps there would be scars for ever. She took a deep breath and dived, her heels kicking up briefly with a flurry of spray, then down, into green depths, swimming strongly, afraid of nothing, floating, going up for breath, breaking surface as they had done hours ago, feeling the sun dazzling on the water, tasting the salt on her lips, turning on her back and floating, facing the sky, eyes closed. Goodbye, Brent, she whispered in her heart. You did change me, although you don't know it.

Nonie's house was perched on high, above a rocky inlet on the east of the island. Donna dreamed about returning there as she lay in bed that night. It was a rambling, single-storey structure, built in the 1950's by her late husband, a distinguished playwright, and she had lived there for nearly thirty years with rare excursions to England. To say that she lived alone would be a misnomer. Nonie had an extensive circle of friends world-wide; artists, writers, actors and actresses, and all were welcome. It was unusual to find her alone. Donna had perhaps been fortunate in that, for when she had fled there—was it only a week ago?—only the staff were in residence with their mistress, which had enabled Donna to pour her heart out unreservedly. Now in the half drifting state preceding the morning's awakening, Donna wondered if that were still the case. Unlikely. . . .

It might be better if there were visitors. Nonie might see too much into her heart, and Donna wasn't quite ready for that—yet. The time to tell would be later. She wondered, as she lay in bed in the pre-dawn time, when the world still slept, if Nonie, with her shrewd perception, might see the change in her, and wonder. Although in her seventies, Nonie, who had never had children of her own, had become a surrogate mother to Donna, as loving, as kind, and as never-questioning as the ideal parent.

She saw far more than anyone Donna had ever met. She blessed the decision, by whichever parent it had been, to choose Nonie for a godmother. It was possibly the most loving thing either of them had ever done in her life. She dozed, and the dreams changed. She was underwater with Brent, in a world much stranger than reality, a world of hidden menace, with mocking laughter following, all around, a nightmare place of voices calling—'spoken like a true Webster'. 'A *true* Webster'—how true!

She turned restlessly and woke up abruptly, heart hammering, and sat up in bed. Sleep had become impossible now. Today they would leave Paradise Island and set course for Barbados, a day and a half journey away, towing her plane, thirty-six hours more. That was all she had: thirty-six hours.

She slipped out of bed, donned her swimsuit and crept out of her cabin. Brent's door was open, silence from within. Very quietly, Donna went to stand outside, then on an impulse she didn't understand, moved silently to peep round the doorway. Brent was fast asleep, lying on his stomach, the sheet kicked off during the night—and he was naked. A pulse beat erratically in her throat at the sight of him lying there, and inside her, warm deep longings stirred, her breathing difficult with the hammer beat of her heart. Oh God, she thought, what a magnificent man! His body was perfect to her eyes; hard and lean and shapely, broad shoulders narrowing to waist and hips, and neat bottom—a strip of white there giving evidence that even when alone, he wore trunks—the briefest possible—thighs and long legs very brown in contrast and tautly muscled—and hairy. Donna couldn't move. *She could not move away*. Even if he woke now, and turned, she doubted she would be capable of movement.

Her mouth had gone dry with the incredible inner warmth that flooded her, her legs shaky. She saw him making love, saw the incredible strength of him, felt as though she were a part of him, a part of that lovemaking. He would be a magnificent animal, aroused, he would be violent and passionate, powerful yet gentle. She knew that, as though he had already made love to her. She had lain with him, here in that very bed, lain beside him and felt that incredible strength—and had felt desire then, but had quashed it because she didn't know how to cope with something she had denied in herself ever since the events of one summer night so many years ago. She knew the final inner truth about herself, and in so doing, found the power of movement, and began to edge backwards. Not cautiously enough. A sound, a mere catching of her heel on carpet—but it woke him, instantly.

One second fast asleep, the next turning, lifting, sitting up. Looking at her. A smile touched his mouth. 'Seen enough?' he asked.

CHAPTER NINE

DONNA's first instinct was for flight—anywhere, but away from him. And that would have been fatal. She took a deep breath instead, keeping her eyes fixed firmly on his ever so slightly mocking face. 'I—came in to tell you I was going for a swim,' she said. It wasn't getting easier by the moment, but at least it wasn't impossible. 'As your door was open, I——' He pulled the sheet, very lazily, over him, which halted her momentarily. 'I—er—assumed you would be respectable,' nice touch that, recalling his words when she had been clad only in a towel in a reverse situation, 'or I wouldn't have *dreamed* of coming in.'

There—at least she had coped with that. 'And as you saw, I wasn't,' he replied, and the amusement had reached his eyes now. Was it just amusement, or was there something else there as well? At least she didn't have to keep her eyes glued on his face. He was covered—partially, but enough.

'Which was why I was going out,' she retorted.

'To knock, and wait, I suppose?' was the dry rejoinder.

'Possibly. I hadn't really given it a thought,' and she shrugged. She would have yawned if she could have managed a convincing one, but he might have thought she was gaping open-mouthed like a fish—and suddenly, belatedly, the humour of the situation struck her. Here was she, a mature woman, acting like an outraged Victorian miss—laughter broke through, and she turned and walked smartly out, and up on deck, still laughing. It was the most effective release from tension that she could have chosen.

She dived into the sea, and as her body hit the water, so the laughter died away. The other impressions remained, and as she swam away from the boat, those were what lingered. The effect that Brent's nude body had had upon her, the dormant desires awoken in her that had never even been touched by any other man; a deep primitive longing for fulfilment that had shaken her beyond anything she had thought possible. She could not have stayed aboard the boat a moment longer. She closed her eyes, drifting with the tide, floating, not wondering any longer why it should have taken her all these years to know the truth, knowing at last. The sea was not yet warm. The cooling effect was precisely what she needed.

She had, ever since that terrifying, accidental encounter years ago, associated making love with all that was frightening; sordid and beastly. And it was not so. In those blinding moments of revelation when she had almost known what it would be like to make love with Brent, she had glimpsed wonders beyond wonders. As though a door, long closed in her mind, had been opened for a brief second to allow her to catch a glimpse of something rich and strange.

Floating in a world of her own, it was a shock to hear water threshing, and approaching, then his voice nearby. 'A good idea, a swim.'

Startled, she turned to see Brent treading water a few feet away, just watching her. 'And as I was dressed for it—nearly—I decided to follow your example,' he said.

Did he mean he was still naked? A glorious sense of

happiness welled up inside her. What did it matter? She had been released from a prison at last. 'Why not? This is my last chance, isn't it?' She swam to be closer to him. Not too near, but nearer.

'Is it?'

'We're leaving today, you said.'

'We don't have to.'

'But I thought——' she stopped.

'You thought what?'

'That you'd have to be on your way to——' she smoothed hair from her eyes, 'to—oh, I don't know, find more treasure. I don't know where you're off to from here——'

'England—eventually,' he responded.

'Yes—well——' Donna was beginning to feel confusion. 'After you've had your boat repaired——'

'After that,' he agreed solemnly. There was a difference in him, in them both, the words banal, said without thought, a making of words on a surface that was eggshell-thin, empty words to hide what lay just beyond that fragile bubble of sound. Donna's heart raced, her body in the cool water grew warmer, an awareness crackled between them that went so deep it was almost frightening. She felt as though he was touching her, touching every hidden part of her, but he wasn't; there was a gap of two or three yards between them. Yet—and yet the sea, caressing her skin, could have been his hands, the heat that struck her cheeks could have been his lips. She turned away, to break the spell because she could not face him. He would see, he would know, with that deep inner perception he possessed.

'I'm in your hands,' she said, realising *what* she had said even as the words came out. She hadn't meant that, she had meant—she didn't know what she had meant.

'Yes, so you are.' He swam beside her, long easy strokes, waves of current travelling from him to her, from her to him. They moved towards the boat as if drawn to it, and their eyes met only briefly.

In silence they climbed aboard, Brent first, reaching down with his hand to help her up.

She walked towards the companionway, her legs suddenly like rubber, her whole body hot with something far greater than the sun's rays. Down the steps, one at a time, slowly, the waiting stillness building up to an explosive strength, no words spoken, none needed. They would have been meaningless anyway, for she could not think. Her mind was a whirl of colour, and images. Her face burned with fire so great she thought she must have a fever. She sought the sanctuary of her cabin, to compose herself, to try and think, to be alone. . . .

Brent walked in with her and she turned to say something, she knew not what, saw his face, saw—saw his eyes, as he moved towards her and took a deep breath. She was aware now of her swimsuit clinging wetly to her, aware that no, he wasn't naked, he wore black briefs, was so aware of him that she could hardly see him.

'I—I was going——' she began, stammering, and he put his finger on her lips.

'No,' he said. 'No, you're not going anywhere.' His hand slid down from her face, down to her shoulders, where he took hold of the thin black strap and eased it down, reached his other hand out and did the same with the other, peeling it down to her waist. He had not taken his eyes from her once. They were darker, they held in them something she had only briefly glimpsed once before. 'We're staying here,' he said, and his eyes travelled slowly to her breasts, and then back. 'Beautiful,' he murmured, the word a caress so deep that she trembled. 'Don't tremble,' he said, the words a whisper of sound, a thread touching her senses, 'you have no need to tremble with me,' and he pulled her gently towards him, into his arms. 'There's no need,' he went on, and eased her swimsuit down again with his right hand, as his left one held her in the small of her back. It lay on the floor and he kicked it away, one movement, gone, then did the same with his own garment.

Then, and only then, did he kiss her, and touch her in a way she had known he would, then he picked her up and carried her to the bed, to lie beside her, his mouth touching her mouth, his hands blazing fire in a sensuous trail across her skin, every inch of her, while Donna lay down, and back, reaching up to touch his face, and he smiled down at her, eyes nearly black with the excitement that could not be spoken—did not need to be put into words, only murmurs, never to be repeated, wonderful whisperings that were a kind of music to her soul. His lips—she had dreamed where those lips would go, she had known, and the reality was a world away from the dreaming, and the reality took her beyond the senses, and beyond reason.

She stirred, she moved, her hands became part of his body; his whispers telling her, guiding her. She needed no guidance, nor did he, and his strength, the strength she knew he possessed, was transmuted into something wonderful, and she gasped, and began to cry out, till he silenced her with his mouth, and with his body answered her unspoken plea. With his body, his warm, wonderful body, he penetrated to the very depths of her being, and she knew only the brief pain of ecstasy in the commencement of the ultimate act, then she was a part of it, and of him, and he of her. Time had no meaning, nor place. She was somewhere far beyond the world, with Brent, somewhere wonderful and indescribable, rhythmic movements, deep pulsating awareness, a rushing onward and onward; she thought she would die. Her brain exploded in a myriad lights, sensations; it could not go on. The pounding roar filled her ears, throbbing sounds—a great cry—then a stillness, a gradual coming down from that place, that paradise, and back into the world.

They were on the boat, they were in her cabin, in her bed. Nearly not in it. Nearly on the floor. Weakly, unable to move more than an inch or two, Donna reached out to pull Brent closer, and she tried to speak, but could not. She could open her eyes, though, and she did, then let out her breath in a deep shuddering sigh.

He kissed her cheek lightly, stroked her thighs, as he lay beside her, and looked at her. Then, very slowly, he smiled and she felt a warm tide of colour rush up into her face. 'I—never—knew——' she said.

'I wouldn't try and talk if I were you,' he said softly. 'I'd save your energy.'

The colour deepened. 'Oh,' she said.

He slid off the bed, looked down at himself, then ruefully at her, and grinned. 'I'm going to get us a drink,' he told her. 'I need one, I don't know about you.' He was gone, and Donna looked at the bed. One pillow on the floor, the sheet hanging off it, the evidence of what had happened imprinted there.

Shakily, holding on to the bed for support, she staggered into her shower room. She saw her face in the mirror and didn't for a moment recognise the wide-eyed gamine, hair tangled, who looked back in astonishment at her. 'My God,' she murmured. 'Oh, my *God*——'

After splashing her body with cool salt water, she made her way back into her cabin. Brent sat in bed drinking a glass of orange juice. 'Here, drink this,' he ordered.

Mindlessly she obeyed, sitting on the edge of the bed, sipping the icy cold juice with gratitude. But she couldn't quite meet his eyes, and after he had put down his glass he took hold of her chin and tilted it so that she faced him. 'Hey—remember me?' he grinned. 'I'm the man you just made love to.'

'I don't think I'll ever be able to forget,' she whispered.

'Come here,' he said, and pulled her towards him.

'Brent!' she gasped. 'I—can't——'

'I can,' he said roughly, 'and I want you again—and soon——' and he kissed her, not gently, but with a kind of savage surprise, as if the thought had excited him beyond measure. 'Oh yes,' he said, 'I want you *now*——'

She had not thought she would have any strength. She certainly had none to resist.

And this time it was different, so very, very different. She knew that by his first movement, by the way his breathing had changed. No longer gentle—but an animal responding to his needs, swifter, deeper, more urgent—and to her own surprise, she found herself responding in kind, panting with her own deeper, newer excitement, answering his greater demands with her own, her body wild and wanton in her responses, her fingers gouging deep into his back with each pounding thrust, both crying out in the urgency of this new and instinctively primitive act of total abandon. Time again became lost, blurred and unknown. With his greater strength and tireless movements, Donna found herself in instinctive tune, her force matching his, her strength naturally the less but her excitement, growing and growing, creating in him greater desire and passion beyond anything that had gone before.

They rolled on to the floor, and the boat rocked with their movement, yet neither was aware of it, rolling over, totally lost. And it was there, after that, they fell asleep together, in a tangle of pillows and sheets. And slept for hours.

Donna took him a cool drink up to the bridge, and stood beside him as he guided the boat through a calm sea. It was late afternoon of the most perfect day of her life, and they were on their way to Barbados.

'Want a turn at the wheel?' he asked.

'I thought you'd never ask.' Brent stood back to sip the drink, as Donna, bracing her legs, took over the wheel, guiding the boat on its journey. She had done this before, many times, on friends' cruisers, but the pleasure had been nothing compared to this. She had no illusions about the source of her happiness. She had been awakened from a sleep of her own making by the man who had shown her that her dreadful guilt feelings were unfounded. He didn't love her, that she knew. He had succumbed to a brief but powerful physical attraction, a combination of setting, opportunity—and, bizarrely—the fact that she had laughed when she had left his cabin, before swimming. Not in words had he told her, but she knew, with her own heightened perception of him, her awareness of so many hidden things about the man. He didn't love her—but she loved him, and she would be grateful to him for the rest of her life—and she couldn't tell him that either.

She was a modern girl, in a modern world. She had no intention of joining in with the 'anything goes' society, but one day, she thought, I shall meet a man who matches up to Brent, and maybe I will learn to love him. Brent was a loner, a man who, by choice, moved in his own way through the world. That much she had gleaned. He was a rare and special man; he had told her more of his life than he probably told anyone before, in that brief period after wakening from their tumultuous lovemaking. She wondered if, even now, he regretted telling her. He had grown up to wealth and privilege, had turned his back on it to do what he wanted, to be a free man. Implicit in the telling, though not said directly, was the need on his part for total freedom—which hadn't tied up, in Donna's mind, with the study, the computer, the link he kept with someone far away. He had laughed, dismissed that as 'keeping an eye on things, no more than that', and changed the subject. She accepted that, how could she not? She saw a man who knew exactly what he was doing. Her love for him was mixed with admiration. She knew the pressures under which her father was placed, the keen cut and thrust of business, the rat race—from which Brent had opted out.

She turned to him now as he returned to the bridge.

after a brief exit. 'I went to check on your plane,' he said, taking her empty glass. 'It's hobbling bravely along behind, like an injured seagull,' which caused her to laugh. Twenty-four precious hours, sharing his kind of freedom, that was all she had. It wasn't enough; an eternity would not be enough, but if it was all she had, then each minute would be precious, gold-filled, to remember for ever. . . .

'If you'd like to take over again, Captain,' she said, 'I'll go and see about making our dinner.'

'And what's it to be?'

'Wait and see.' Something very special for our last dinner together. Tomorrow I'll dine at Nonie's and he'll be gone. So tonight will be special.

'Sounds promising.' He turned and looked at her. 'Give me a shout when it's nearly done, and we'll drop anchor.'

And we'll dine on deck, she thought—by candlelight. The plans were forming, becoming more crystal clear by the moment. What a thought! She had a lot of work to do, and the prospect was a pleasing one. Oh God, I do love you, she thought, and perhaps something shone in her eyes as she answered: 'And you're not to peep until I call you—promise?' For she saw something disturbing and unknown in his own eyes as he nodded.

'I promise.'

First she had to check the place. It had to be just right. In the bows, where there was a large area of deck, near the companionway would be ideal. There was a card table in the main saloon, and two suitable chairs. But she wouldn't take them up until the last moment, in case Brent came down from the bridge for anything. He was not to know until all was perfect and

ready. And if she could persuade him to take a
photograph, she would have something else to
remember of her trip to paradise. . . .

She went into the galley to begin preparations.
First, the freezer compartment of the refrigerator. The
large chicken she had bought was there, rock-hard.
Out to thaw on a convenient working top, then she
crouched down and began to sort through the
crammed selection of fresh vegetables therein, selecting
her choice with care, a song in her heart, her entire
being concentrating on preparing a meal that he too
might remember. And if he doesn't, it won't be my
fault, she thought.

It was dark when at last she carried the card table
up on deck, followed by the two chairs. She laid
over the table the large multi-coloured silk stole she
had popped into her luggage as a fortuitous
afterthought, and it was perfect. She stood back to
look at it, but for only a second; there was too much
to be done to stand round admiring her handiwork.
There was a candle to be found, and lit, unfortunately not a red one, a rather prosaic white
tallow candle, but she had had an idea about that
too. She ran down again to the galley, found the
store of candles, selected one and borrowed Brent's
lighter to melt its base to a saucer. She removed the
purple and silver paper from a bar of chocolate in
the refrigerator and, with skilful fingers, made it into
a pretty decoration at the base of the candle. That
would be lit at the last moment. She carried that up
with the cutlery and condiments and set them in
place on the transformed card table.

Music! Yes, of course. The speakers had long leads.

She placed them both strategically at the foot of the steps, put on a long-playing tape of the Bruch and Mendelssohn violin concertos, then ran up again to check that it could be heard. It could—beautifully, not so near as to be an intrusion, but a background accompaniment. She ran down again, thinking as she did so, I should be losing pounds with all this exercise, switched it off and went back into the galley. The chicken was tender, skin crisply brown, bubbling in its own juices with roast potatoes and onions surrounding it. Peas in a pan ready to be heated at the last moment, apple sauce cooling, a rich gravy filled with mushrooms simmering gently next to the peas. A bottle of wine cooled in the refrigerator.

She had scooped the seeds from two halves of a melon, poured in kirsch, and left it to stand. Everything was nearly ready for the guest of honour.

Donna whipped off the tea-towel she had used as an apron, showered in twenty seconds flat—she timed it—and donned her green dress, then ran up again to the bridge. 'It's nearly ready,' she told him, 'but you're to close your eyes on deck. I'll guide you down.'

'Really?' He raised one eyebrow in surprise. 'I am intrigued.'

'Yes, so you should be,' she smiled mysteriously.

'Okay.' He switched off the engines, pressed a button, and she heard the anchor chain clanking below as it was released to go to the bottom of the sea bed. 'Lead on, Vice-Captain. I'm yours to command.' He followed her down the steps and when she reached deck she turned.

'Close your eyes now, and hold my hand.' Looking amused and faintly puzzled, Brent obeyed, and she led him down, past the table, guided him by the speakers, led him to his cabin and opened the door. 'Now, you have ten minutes to do whatever it is you have to do,' she told him. 'Then I'll shout you when it's all ready, and take you up.'

'Yours to command,' he agreed amiably, and she closed his door and went back grinning to the galley.

She switched on the tape, ran up with the melon and wine, lit the candle, and looked round. There was no land to be seen anywhere, just the deep purpley black sea all around, with the moon lighting a silver path along it. The setting was perfect, and Donna's heart filled with a strange mixture of happy-sadness. Everything was beautiful, so beautiful that it hurt. For a brief hour or two, this beauty would be theirs, to capture in memory, to be recalled when Brent was long gone from her life. The music swelled and rose in the background, yet soft, as heart-achingly beautiful as the sea around them and matching its mood of serene wonder. Tears came to her eyes and she blinked them away, and went down to take him to the table.

Eyes closed, hand holding hers, he followed her up, and when they reached the table she said softly: 'You can open your eyes now.'

He did. For a moment he said nothing, just looked, at the table with its soft-hued multi-coloured cloth, candle gleaming in accompaniment to the moon's paler light, melon, bottle of wine, gleaming cutlery, then he sighed. 'You're a witch—this is quite magical.'

'Then please be seated,' she told him, as she did so. He poured out the wine for them both, raised his glass, and added:

'Thank you for all your work. Your good health, Donna.'

'And yours. And—thank you for letting me find myself at last.'

He smiled. 'Don't give me credit where it's not due. You'd have done it anyway.'

'Perhaps.' She smiled back at him. The candlelight softened his face, blurred the hard planes. He looked gentle, but he looked all man, always would. The faintest of cool breezes flickered the flame, making it dance for a moment or two, and he was right, it *was* magical. The melon was superb, and when it was finished she took the plates away and returned only minutes later with the main course.

Brent looked down at the plate she set in front of him and drew in his breath. 'My God, you've excelled yourself here!' He looked across at her.

'Then eat, and enjoy it.' She sipped her wine. 'Brent, would it be possible to take a photograph of us eating?'

'Now, you mean? Certainly.'

'No, after this. There's cheese and grapes to follow. During that. Oh, and coffee, of course.'

'And liqueurs.'

'Naturally,' she murmured, and her smile turned to laughter, bubbling up helplessly. 'I'll remember this for a long time.' She didn't say 'for ever', it wasn't necessary.

'So will I,' he agreed softly. 'So will I.' Donna wondered if he meant it. He wasn't given to flowery phrases—no, she wouldn't expect that. He was a man who spoke his mind—forcefully if need be—but for now, just for a few precious hours, he was different, and the difference showed, and made her happier than she had ever thought could be possible. And it wouldn't matter if we were eating just bread and drinking water, she thought, the same magic would be here.

Everything was delicious, as she had so carefully prepared and hoped for, the chicken succulent, vegetables and gravy melt-in-the-mouth, the setting a perfect foil for them both.

Time passed, in a golden dream; Donna went to make coffee and Brent to fetch his camera, set it on a tripod, and when it was ready they faced the camera with glasses raised, candle between them gleaming, and he took not one but a dozen photographs and told her he would develop them that very night.

And at last, at long last, the lovely dinner was finished, every last bite, and they both cleared away and switched off the music, and when Donna went to wash up, he took her in his arms and kissed her. 'No,' he said, 'I'll do that—but in the morning,' and they both knew exactly what he meant, which was not the same as his words, and their eyes met for a brief moment, and Donna nodded.

'Yes,' she said. 'Of course.' She added: 'I'm in your hands.'

They were nearing Barbados when the accident happened. Brent was on the bridge, the boat cutting through the water at a fair speed, and Donna went to have a shower. The boat gleamed, everything shipshape, for she had worked hard that morning after a night—their very last night together—spent in his arms. Her heart ached with a pain that grew stronger as each hour passed. She had wanted desperately to ask him to go to Nonie's with her, but, strangely for her, she couldn't find the words. She knew she must not. He would never be possessed, by her or perhaps not by any woman. It would have to be someone very special to capture his heart. She wondered how he would say goodbye, and where. After he had taken her plane back with her? Would he shake her hand, and say: 'That's it, I'm off. See you around some time?'

No, he wouldn't do it like that. But whatever, it would be goodbye.

She picked up the half dozen photographs to pack in her case. They were good and sharply defined, the candle flame a small halo lighting their faces, both smiling, glasses winking in the flash, a memory captured for ever in one frozen second of time. She placed them carefully in her case, then looked around her. Not much more to do now, only bundle up her sheets and towels, and wash them. They would dry in no time over the rails.

She washed them and was going up on deck with the dripping bundle, her vision obscured, when she caught her foot in a trailing sheet and fell the full length of the steps to the bottom, the wet sheets trumbling after her. For a moment she lay winded at the foot of the stairs, the breath knocked from her body, then she tried to move. She had given herself a nasty knock, landed on her back, was slightly dizzy, but struggled to her feet—tried to walk, and collapsed in pain as her ankle gave way. She didn't cry out, but gritted her teeth, biting back tears. The pain was intense, making her feel quite sick. Sitting, Donna pulled the scattered bundle of wet washing to her, grabbed the smaller of the two towels and wrapped it round her foot, which lessened the agony, but only fractionally.

Brent wouldn't hear her above the noise of the engines even if she called as loudly as she could. But she needed him—oh, how she needed him! Very slowly, each step jarring her body with renewed pain, she dragged herself up by the rail, and hopping, began to mount the steps. She was nearly fainting by the time she reached deck, everything swirling round alarmingly, but she hung on grimly to the rail and made her slow tortuous way along, along, each step achieved a major triumph, until she was near enough to shout his name, a long, despairing cry of: 'Brent—please help! Brent——'

He heard, she saw his face looking down, saw the state she was in, and the next moment the sound of the engines died away and he was leaping down, coming towards her, as ashen-faced, trembling, she waited.

'What happened?' he demanded.

'I fell down the—the steps——' He picked her up, said:

'Don't talk, let's get you in your cabin——' and began to walk back towards the companionway. Donna saw his face through the mists of pain that obscured her vision. She thought she must be suffering from delirium as well as whatever else—for she thought she saw, for one brief second, an expression of pleasure, it was nothing so definite as a smile—merely a fleeting impression, so quickly vanished that it must have been her imagination. For how could he be pleased at what had happened?

CHAPTER TEN

BRENT soaked a roll of bandage in iced water and wrapped it tightly round her ankle. She sat on her bed while he did it, and never made a sound even though the pain was intense. He looked up at her white face at one stage. 'Does it hurt much?' he asked.

She nodded, mouth tightly shut, teeth clenched, and he added: 'If it's any consolation, I don't think it's broken—but a bad sprain can sometimes be worse than a break.'

'Thanks,' she gritted.

'I've got some painkillers that will make you sleepy—they're very effective, though. And you'd better lie on my bed—it's more comfortable.' He indicated the bare mattress, the uncovered pillow.

'No. We're nearly in Barbados——'

'So?'

'I—want—we must——' she didn't know what it was she wanted. Except him.

'Where does your godmother live?' he asked.

'On the north east side of the land—you can land the boat—it's right on the sea——' She had closed her eyes; she didn't see his face when she said that. She would have been even more confused if she had.

'We'll go straight there,' he said.

Donna opened her eyes. 'But you——'

'No buts. Do you think I'd leave you to stagger there on your own from Bridgetown? Don't be an idiot!'

A little tear trickled down her cheek and he stood

up, lifted and carried her to his cabin, set her down on the bed and said: 'I won't be a minute.'

'The sheets——'

'I'll see to those as well. Lie down, stay there and shut up.' With that he went out, and Donna did as she was told. It was easier that way. When he returned he handed her two white tablets and a glass of water. 'Take those now,' he said. 'They won't knock you out, I promise, but they'll make you drowsy.'

She put them in her mouth, grimaced at the bitter salt taste, then swallowed them with a draught of water and lay back again. Her ankle throbbed, swollen like a balloon. Of all the stupid, idiotic things to have done, she thought. To be so near—and then, and only then, did the significance of Brent's words strike her. He was going to Nonie's after all. Not by choice, but necessity. But he *was* going. It wouldn't be goodbye in Bridgetown—not immediately. Her heart did a ridiculous little flip, and she even managed to smile.

He would surely stay for one night at the least. She wanted Nonie to meet him, and she would. She desperately wanted Nonie to like him. It was very important. He was standing by the window, looking out, an air of deep thought around him, then he turned. 'Did you say it was your godmother who'd told you about the island?'

Donna frowned, caught unawares by the question. 'Yes.' Then she added: 'Why?'

He shrugged. 'I just wondered.'

The pills were certainly fast working. She felt as she did after a stiff vodka, pleasantly muzzy. He saw. He sees everything, she thought, then—no, he doesn't, thank the Lord. Not everything, or he'd know how I feel, and he'd run a mile, sprained ankle or no. 'I'll leave you and we'll get under way,' he said. 'The pain will go, I assure you.'

'I believe you—my head's quite pleasantly light. I feel as though I'm drunk.'

Brent laughed as he went out and she heard him pause at the foot of the steps, presumably to gather up her washing, then ascending. A few minutes after that, the engines started up. They were on their way again.

She was dimly aware that the engines had stopped, that there was the unmistakable and boat-shaking sound of chains unwinding at high speed, but it didn't have any great significance. Then footsteps, near, nearer, Brent coming in, looking at her. 'Ready to go?' he asked.

'Where? Why have we stopped?'

'Because we've arrived.' He bent and picked her up. She thought—I must have dozed after all. I didn't think I would. The pain was a dull throb, bearable and no more than uncomfortable, and she told him so as she put her arms round his neck. As they reached deck she looked to land, and there, perched high on the hill, was Golden Haven, with the long winding row of steps carved in the rock leading down to the beach. In a few minutes they would see Nonie. She clung to Brent tightly as he climbed down the ladder—no easy exercise, that, for him—and waded to shore, carrying her as easily as he would a baby. The late afternoon sun slanted on the rich profusion of trees, dappling them in gold and black, and she could hear distant music, as if in welcome. She looked back towards the boat, sheets draped over the rails, her plane bobbing a distance behind it, and wondered what Nonie would make of *that*, and wanted to laugh, or cry, she wasn't sure which.

Brent began the steep ascent, taking it slowly, pausing for a few moments every twenty steps or so. And it still hadn't struck her. It was as they neared the top, the last dozen steps, and the music was louder, a Beatles record of all things, 'Sergeant Pepper's Lonely Hearts Club Band'—quite catchy, ideal for carrying stupid women with sprained ankles up *thousands* of steps with—it was *then* that she realised what should have been blindingly obvious half an hour ago, and she gasped:

'But how did you *know*?'

'Know what?'

'That we were *here*—that—this was Nonie's house?'

'Isn't it?' They had reached the top and he stopped. His forehead glistened with perspiration, their bodies were damp where they touched.

'Yes, but——'

'Wait. You'll have your question answered in a moment.' His eyes, his face were giving nothing away. Then Donna turned her head at a cry from the terrace, saw the small white-haired woman who was moving out to them, and she called out:

'Nonie! Oh—Nonie,' voice catching with emotion, and Nonie, near them now, answered:

'Donna, my darling—what on *earth*——' then paused, adding, in a tone holding great surprise: 'And *Brent*! My dear boy, what are you doing here after all this time?'

Donna could scarcely believe what was happening. Nonie knew Brent! She *knew* him. He was putting her down on a terrace seat, was turning, kissing the sweet-faced elderly woman, was saying something, but Donna didn't hear. She was too numbed with shock to take anything in. Then Nonie was kissing and hugging

ıer, and Donna clung to her for a few moments, to try
ınd get her bearings. To try and understand what was
ıappening.

'You know Brent?' she managed to say at last. Brent
tood a few feet away, flexing his hands, doubtless
ching after a marathon climb, not speaking but
vatching, hard to tell what were his thoughts.
Certainly his face gave nothing away.

'My dear, I've known him longer than I've known
ou! What *I* want to know is how come you're
ogether. This is impossible! Somebody explain to me
ılease, what is *happening*!' Nonie sat down next to
Donna, looking up in apparent bewilderment at the
ilent man, who smiled a rare smile and answered:

'Why, Aunt *Nemone*, we bumped into each other on
ın island far away, set in a magic sea. And Donna told
ıe about her godmother whose name was *Nonie*—and
ı wasn't until a few hours ago that I realised it was
ou.'

'I couldn't say Nemone when I was a child——'
Donna began, to be interrupted by the old woman's
oot of laughter. She banged her stick on the ground,
ıntranced with the explanation.

'Incredible! Quite remarkable! This calls for a
rink. Champagne, I think. Brent, my darling boy, go
ı and shout William, will you?' She laid her hand on
Donna's. 'And you, my darling, what have you done
ıat requires a strong man to carry you here?' She
egarded Donna's ankle with a frown.

Donna explained hastily. She wanted to know how
Ionie knew the man she loved, and he would be back
ny minute. 'Nonie,' she began, 'you know Brent—but
ow?'

Her godmother chuckled. 'His grandfather and my

dear Charles were school friends way, way back. He'
told you about his grandfather, of course?'

'No. I know nothing—or *next* to nothing——' sh
corrected herself, 'about him.'

'Good gracious! Don't you? And I know every
thing——' Nonie too corrected herself, impishly—'o
nearly everything about him. His grandfather on hi
mother's side, Henry Russell, founded the Russel
empire. You've surely heard of Russell's Electronics?

The last pieces of a jigsaw that had puzzled Donn
for days fell neatly into place. Her godmother's word
explained the computer aboard Brent's boat, explaine
the apparent ease with which a computer salesman—
ye gods! she had thought him a *salesman!*—coul
travel the world on a whim without fear of losing hi
job. He, Brent, quite possibly owned Russell'
Electronics, one of the big five British companie
manufacturers of a good third of all British-mad
computers, televisions and videos, and wieldin
immense power in industry. 'My God,' she sai
shaken. 'He never said.'

'Well, he wouldn't, would he, my darling?' the ol
woman murmured, a glint in her eye. 'Brent is one c
the very few people I know to whom money is no
remotely interesting, either for spending or as a topi
of conversation. The last time I saw him—in Englan
it was, about eight years ago, he'd just returned from
walking trip in Tibet—he had a beard a foot lon;
wore disgusting jeans and boots that looked as thoug
he had walked every foot of the way—and he was :
happy as a sandboy!'

Donna could believe that with ease. She though
with an inward shudder, of the crass way she ha
treated him when first they met. He had demolishe

her then, with well chosen words, richly deserved, and knew, with a sense of recognition, that he had taught her something else valuable: humility. It was another thing to add to the growing list in her mind. Her godmother, perhaps seeing her troubled eyes, smiled gently. 'You like him very much, don't you?'

'Does it show so clearly?' Donna asked softly— then heard him returning, and put a forefinger to her lips. Nonie nodded, understanding, and both women turned to watch him come out. He carried a silver bucket, ice-filled, in which nestled a bottle of champagne. He also carried three glasses. The suspicions were too great in Donna's mind to allow her to remain silent. She looked at Nonie, whose sweet innocent face was as guileless as a baby's. 'Did you know Brent would be on Paradise Island when you told me to go there?' she asked, and the question was greeted with a shocked silence until Brent broke it.

'I can explain that, I think,' he said, busily engaged in easing the cork from the bottle. 'Nonie's husband— may call you Nonie too, may I?' he received a nod of assent from the amused elderly woman, 'Charles and my grandfather, Henry, came here many years ago, set off exploring and "discovered" Paradise Island—and I heard about it when I was very young. And they too had heard of the wrecked ship—a rumour, no more, but I did the investigating, when I got the taste for exploration in my blood, and found out that it perhaps wasn't the fairy story they'd imagined it to be, after all.' The cork soared skywards, the fizzy spume frothed out and he tipped it into a glass, all in one deft movement. Nonie clapped her hands.

'Well done! And did you find it—the treasure, I
mean?'

He passed them each a glass. 'Oh yes, I did—or
rather, we did, Donna and I.' He raised his glass to
her. 'Let's drink to the reunion of old friends and a
successful venture.' His eyes were on Donna as he
spoke, and she felt herself grow warm. She raiséd her
own glass in response and sipped the dry cold
champagne, delicious after a long journey. The ideal
end, in fact.

'Oh, it's so *lovely* to see you both,' Nonie smiled.
'And such a delightful coincidence!'

'Indeed it is,' Brent responded, his tone as dry as
the champagne, and Donna watched him, but
remained silent. She was happy, and puzzled, and a lot
of other confused things all rolled into one—and her
foot was starting to ache quite painfully again, but not
for anything would she spoil the magic of this
moment.

It was Nonie who saw, who looked at her face and
then made a small imperceptible sign to Brent, who
put down his glass and said: 'I think it might be a
good idea to have a doctor look at your foot, Donna.'

'Yes, I think so, too,' Nonie agreed. 'I'll go and
telephone now. Excuse me.' She rose to her feet and
went indoors, trailing silken scarves. She usually wore
long robes of cotton or silk, invariably exotically
patterned and coloured. She was a bright, wonderful
person who extended her own aura of vitality and love
and would have looked good if she had worn a flour
sack. A scarf floated to the ground, and Brent went to
pick it up and put it over the back of her chair, and he
wasn't smiling, not exactly; it was hard to tell what he
was thinking, but Donna could imagine.

'You don't think——' she began.

'That Nonie had anything to do with the little "coincidence"?' he finished drily. 'I don't know. Do you?'

'No—or at least, *I* certainly didn't!' It seemed important to reassure him on that point.

'I didn't imagine *that* for a moment. Our mutual surprise was something that couldn't have been made up.' He looked at Donna. 'But Nonie could out-manoeuvre Machiavelli at his best if she so decided.' Then he smiled. 'She really is an incredible woman.'

'I'll drink to that,' said Donna, lifting her glass. A twinge of severe pain smote her, and the glass shook, and Brent, seeing, said:

'Take a couple more of these,' and produced the pills from his shorts pocket.

'Hadn't I better wait for the doctor?'

'Not necessary. Here.' He handed her the bottle and she opened it, as Nonie returned, beaming.

'He'll be along in half an hour, then we'll dine. Oh, my children, won't it be *lovely*!'

Floating away into a drug-induced sleep that night, Donna thought: I don't care if Nonie did work some scheme—and she wondered if she would ever know the truth. She had gone to bed leaving them talking on the terrace. Her room was a distance away, but their voices floated along diffused into murmurs in the night air, and it was an effort to think properly, thoughts dissolving, images changing, a struggle to keep awake. She heard a man's laughter and smiled faintly to herself. Her ankle was firmly bandaged, she had been told to rest it as much as possible for at least a week, and she wondered, in the moments before sleep claimed her, if Brent would stay for a day or two. Then she slept.

She awoke to the song of birds and the sight of bright sunshine streaming in through her window, and felt incredibly good. There was a tap on her door, and she wondered if that was what had woken her, and called: 'Come in.' It was Brent, carrying a breakfast tray, freshly shaved and dressed most respectably in fine cream trousers and white short-sleeved shirt.

'Good morning,' he said. 'How's the foot?'

'Better, thanks.' She sat up and smiled at him. He sat on the side of the bed and helped himself to a piece of her toast.

'Good. I'm going to take your plane and my boat this morning. I'll need your papers, Donna.'

'Of course. They're in my tote-bag——' it was by the side of her bed. She leaned over and picked it up. 'You'll let me know any further charges, won't you?'

'I will.'

'Have you eaten?' He nodded, finished off her piece of toast, looked wistfully at the second, then stood up.

'Yes. Nonie and I ate on the terrace a while back. It's nearly noon.'

'Good grief!' There was no clock in the bedroom, and Donna's watch had stopped at three o'clock. The hours were too precious to waste in sleep, but it was too late to worry about that. 'I'll get up.'

'Slowly, mind. And sit with your feet up.'

'Yes, doctor,' she retorted, and stuck out her tongue. Brent smiled as he went towards the door.

'I'll be a couple of hours. I'm taking my boat for repair—see you later.' He was gone, and the room seemed less bright. Donna finished her breakfast, then hobbled to the bathroom for a shower. She hoped his boat would take several days to repair. Or even weeks, but that might be being a little too greedy, she decided. Now was what mattered, and the quality of now. And her other world receded still further. Of Steven she had not thought at all, for days.

She put on a simple yellow sun-dress after her shower, then went to find Nonie. Her godmother was dozing on the terrace in the shade of a lime tree, feet up on a footstool, a cool drink at her side on the table. Gentle snores arose, and Donna, grinning, sat down very quietly opposite and edged her foot on to the stool. The warm scented air was humid, and her hair was damp with perspiration in minutes. Nonie was used to it. She always looked cool. Perhaps, thought Donna, she knows something I don't, with her long silky kaftans. She would go into Bridgetown when she was able and buy one or two. Nonie had a car, driven by William, the general factotum, whose wife Esmeralda kept house, and when guests were there, was assisted by two of her four daughters. They had been with Nonie for as long as Donna could remember, lived in their own house in the extensive grounds, and were a warmhearted couple. Donna had great affection for them both.

The old woman stirred, opened her eyes and said accusingly: 'Why didn't you tell me you were there?'

'I was enjoying listening to your gentle snores!' Donna teased.

Nonie snorted. 'Me, snoring? I *never* snore!'

'Of course not!'

'Brent's gone to Bridgetown. He'll phone when he's ready and William will meet him with the car.'

'Can I go down with him, then? I've decided I'd like to buy one or two kaftans like yours—you always look so cool.'

'You can't go to the shops in that condition!' Nonie sounded shocked.

'The doctor said I had to rest. He didn't say I had to stay totally immobile, godmother dear,' Donna protested. 'I can borrow one of your many walking sticks if it makes you feel better.'

'See what Brent says when he phones, then,' answered Nonie, and Donna raised her eyebrows.

'He's taking over, is he?' She mimicked her godmother's words: 'See what *Brent* says,' and was rewarded with a rap on her hand from Nonie's stick.

'That's quite enough cheek, young lady.' Nonie grinned like a mischievous child. 'Mind you, you're quite right. He *does* rather take over wherever he goes.' You can say that again, thought Donna.

'I remember once,' she began, an inevitable prelude to a rambling anecdote, to which Donna would always listen with interest, whether feigned or not—but now, whatever Nonie said would be fascinating, because it was going to be about Brent, and there would never be enough to hear as far as Donna was concerned. 'Once when he was here—just for a few days, you understand, he's always on the move, a restless spirit is our Brent—where was I?' she frowned.

'You were saying,' Donna prompted, 'that once when he was staying here——'

'Ah yes. I do digress at times, don't I? Well, it was—oh, let me see, about ten years ago, he'd have been in his early twenties then and fresh down from Cambridge, and his father still at the head of the firm, so Brent had no responsibilities, which made a difference, anyway, he landed here late one night in his boat—not the same one, I don't imagine, and there'd been terrible storms a day or so previously, the telephone lines were down, we had no electricity, no running water and were living like primitive cave men—poor William was doing his best, and he's a dear, but not mechanically minded, and you know what it's like trying to get workmen when you want them, especially as most of the rest of the island was in the same stew. Well! He *erupted* on to the scene, took one look around and summed up the situation, stripped off to the waist and got cracking on the electricity repairs for a start, took the car to Bridgetown and brought back two very dazed-looking plumbers, and in less than twenty-four hours had everything back in working order. He's like a dynamo when he gets going!'

Donna had listened, fascinated by every word. But something struck her.

'Nonie,' she asked, 'doesn't he need *people*? Is he always alone?'

A strange look came into the other's eyes. 'He is a loner—now. But he hasn't always been—oh, dear me no! But he's changed, ever since Laura—he's changed.'

'Laura?' A pang of something terrible smote Donna. Deeper than jealousy, it was almost frightening.

'He hasn't told you? No, he wouldn't.' Nonie's eyes were far away, looking somewhere very distant. 'He brought her here once, a beautiful girl, and it was obvious that he was deeply in love with her—and she with him. I think they were planning to get married. Only——' she paused, 'something went wrong, I never did find out what, and when next I saw him, it broke my heart. It was as if the life had gone out of him, that vital force he exudes had vanished. He never spoke about it, and he never mentioned her name.

Then I heard that she'd died, been killed in a plane crash somewhere in Australia. Brent flew out there for her funeral, and when he came back, started to work in the firm for a time, until he was off again on his travels. And that's how he's been ever since. Yes, my dear, in answer to your question, he's a loner. And suppose, he always will be. Some men are like that. She patted Donna's hand, her eyes filled with sad tears. 'I think you love him very much, don't you?'

Donna nodded. 'Yes, I do,' she whispered.

Nonie sighed. 'He's a wonderful man, I too love him dearly. And the odd thing, I've never realised before—but Laura could have been your twin. There's a great likeness there.' She closed her eyes, her face sad. Donna sat there, and for a few moments her mind was numb. She had thought, when Brent had made love to her, that it was because of an overwhelming physical need. Perhaps so. But could there have been deeper, far more complex reason? Could he, perhaps have thought he was possessing Laura? Could it have been *her* he had been thinking of when he was making love to Donna? Sick at heart, she gazed almost unseeing at the old woman opposite her, and for moment she hated Brent. What was it Nonie had said—he was deeply in love with her—perhaps he still was.

CHAPTER ELEVEN

WHEN Brent returned, Donna was outwardly her normal self, but something inside her had died. Perhaps there had been a small hope in her that one day he might love her—a small never to be spoken, scarcely even to be thought, hope. That was what had died, yet Donna was scarcely aware of it. But more, and strangely, he was different. Something had changed in him. Heightened perception made her aware of something not quite right, and once, when she turned unexpectedly when they were on the terrace, he was looking at her in a way that caused her heart to pound in sudden—sudden fear. It took her by surprise. She had nothing to fear from Brent. And yet there was an unease in her. It was as if he might have overheard their conversation and was angry—no, absurd, it couldn't be that. But there had been such gravity in his face, such a dark seriousness in his eyes as to make her feel strange—and as though he himself were a stranger.

He knew she had seen, because he spoke then, voice light. 'If you really want to go shopping, Donna, perhaps tomorrow? I just didn't think you were well enough today. What say you, Nonie?'

'I agree with *you*, Brent,' responded the old lady, eyes glinting. She was totally unaware of Donna's inner distress, that was clear. 'But then I always do. It makes life easier,' and she chuckled.

He bent to kiss her cheek. 'You said that so

convincingly I almost believed it,' he told her. 'And the day you feel obliged to agree, for the sake of peace with anything I or anyone else says is the day I'll give up.'

Nonie leaned up to pat the hand that rested on her shoulder. 'Oh, it does my heart good to have you here. How long can you stay?' It was the question Donna could not ask. She caught her breath.

'How long do you want me?'

'As long as you like. Do you need to even *ask*?'

'No, of course. Well, for a few days at least. My boat won't be ready until Friday, that's two days, and I have no urgent appointments anywhere, so——' he shrugged, 'if you'll have me, I'll stay here. I can make myself useful. And I've not shown you our little haul yet, have I? It's in my room—excuse me.' He strode away, and Donna and Nonie exchanged glances.

'Well,' whispered the old woman, 'did I ask the question you wanted to ask?'

'Yes,' Donna nodded. But would it be the same now, knowing what she did? Why was everything so—different? Something else happened only minutes later that caused her to feel yet more uneasy. Brent had returned with the blue cloth bundle, and set it out on the table in front of Nonie, and while she was admiring the jewellery, totally enraptured, he said:

'You do have a burglar alarm system, don't you Nonie?' The old woman looked up, surprised.

'Why, yes, but we rarely use it—why, Brent? Surely——' she indicated the pile of gleaming gold and silver—'these aren't worrying you?'

He shrugged. 'Oh, I'd sleep better if it was on.' Donna looked at him. This surely was not Brent speaking? Brent? Nervous of burglars? She felt as she was going mad. What was it? She did not even think of the most logical explanation of all. It was not until much later that evening that she discovered the truth. And when she did, when Brent told her and she understood the change in him, it was yet another blow to her already shocked system.

It happened after dinner. They had eaten late, and Nonie, uncharacteristically, had pleaded tiredness and said she was going to have an early night, if they would excuse her. After she had gone, Donna and Brent remained on the terrace, their coffee growing cold on the table. Brent was smoking a cheroot, and Donna's heart contracted in sudden pain as she watched him. So near, and yet so far. He was with her, and yet somewhere far away. She could no longer help herself. 'Brent,' she began, voice heistant, unsure of herself, 'what is it? Please tell me. Is it something I've said or done?'

For the first time in several hours, he smiled. 'No. Was I that obvious? If so, I apologise.' He crushed the half-smoked cheroot out into an ashtray, regarded her across the table, seemed about to speak when William walked out, soft-footed, bearing a tray with fresh coffee.

'Excuse me, Mr Sanders,' he began, 'but would it be all right if we went to bed now? I've brought you more coffee.'

'Thanks, William,' Brent seemed somewhat relieved at the other's interruption, 'just what we needed. No, you go. I'll lock up.'

'Thank you, then—goodnight, sir, goodnight, Miss Donna.'

He put the coffee down, removed the old pot and used cups, as both Donna and Brent bade him goodnight, and vanished into the house. Donna turned the clean cups the right way up in their saucers and began to pour for them both. Her foot had started to ache; so had her head. She felt more unsure of herself at that moment than she had done for a very long time. What did she say now? Was he going to tell her what was wrong? Was he going to tell her about Laura? She felt real apprehension, slowly building as each moment ticked past, and her knuckles were white as she gripped the table.

Brent looked at her. 'I don't know how to put this gently,' he said. 'There's only one way to say it. Steven is here in Barbados.' For a moment she felt only relief. Was *that* all? She had feared far worse——

'He telephoned Nonie a few days ago—she told me last night, after you'd gone to bed, hadn't wanted to worry you—and she told me he sounded distraught. She told him that she had no idea where you were, and as far as she was concerned, that was that.'

'Oh, Brent!' Donna let out her breath in a long sigh. 'Is that what was troubling you? You have no need, I assure you. I'm not frightened of Steven. In fact, I feel almost sorry for him.' I know what it feels like now, to love and not be loved in return, she thought, but I can't tell you that. 'I'll see him and tell him——'

'That's not quite all,' he cut in. 'And Nonie doesn't know this next bit. When I took the plane back, they told me a man had been asking after you, had showed them your photograph, had offered them money to let him know immediately the plane was returned. He won't be put off that easily, unfortunately, I think it's quite possible he'll turn up here.'

'And that's why you're staying?'

He nodded. 'Yes.'

'And that's also why you asked about the burglar alarm?'

'It seems a sensible precaution,' he answered drily.

Donna closed her eyes for a moment, relief and confusion blending in her mind. Brent was staying—for her sake. That was a warming thought, yet followed by another: he was worried about Steven—and Brent was surely the last man to worry about anything without good reason.

'Brent, I hate to say it, but I think you're being—rather over-cautious—I appreciate your concern, truly I do, but——' she shrugged, 'I *have* changed. I can see Steven in perspective now. He's just a rather over-zealous suitor—I can cope.'

'No,' said Brent, voice quiet. 'No, I don't think you can.' And she was sobered by what she saw in his face, in his eyes, and she went very still.

'You think he's out to cause trouble?' Her voice no more than a whisper.

'If my instincts are right—and I trust them—yes, I do.'

'Then—what do I do?'

'What do *we* do, you mean?' There was all the world in that one different word. All the difference in the world. I don't hate you, she thought. Could I even for a moment have thought I did? I love you so much, and you will never know, and you are strong and true, and Laura must have been a very special woman.

'Yes,' she whispered.

'I think we do something very simple, Donna. Something that will enable *me* to deal with him effectively and finally. We tell him we're engaged to be married.'

His words had the strangest effect on her. For a moment she couldn't speak. She tried, but words refused to come. By his next words, it was obvious that he had misunderstood her silence. 'It's not all that absurd, is it?' low-voiced, something deeper, beyond that, almost a harshness. If only he knew!

She breathed deeply, calming herself. 'It sounds very sensible, Brent. I was just—taken aback, that's all.' She finished her coffee and lifted the pot to see if there was more, pleased at how steady her hand was. 'More coffee?'

'Please.'

'Cream?'

'Just a little.'

'I have a ring,' Donna began. 'It belonged to my mother——'

'Then wear it, tomorrow, will you?'

'Yes, I will, of course.' She looked around her, at the darkness surrounding them, and for the first time since he had spoken she felt the first twinges of fear. Suppose Steven were out there now, waiting, listening? It was an absurd fancy to have, yet she could not shake it off. Brent saw her looking, and said quietly:

'Do you want to go inside?'

'I think—yes.'

'You're quite safe, you know.' He didn't add, 'with me,' he didn't need to.

She finished the drink, and stood up and Brent followed suit. She had borrowed one of Nonie's sticks, and she picked it up from the chair and began to walk painfully towards the house. Brent put his hand on her arm, and together they walked indoors, he pausing to lock the terrace door after them and check it. 'Wait,' he said, 'I'll make sure everything else is secured.' And he strode away, leaving her standing in the darkened drawing room, wondering why he had told her to wait. He was back in a minute, and took her arm. 'I'll make sure your window is secure,' he told her.

They walked together along the wide hallway and into the passage leading to their adjoining rooms. 'What about Nonie's window?' she asked him.

'I've already fixed that, before she went to bed. It can only be opened a foot. Not enough for anyone to get in.' They were at her door now. He opened it, and Donna went in, and his quietly spoken words had an effect different from what he intended. They were practical words, yet she shivered, cold despite the warmth of the night air.

'You're really serious, aren't you?' she said. 'You think he would try to get in——'

'I'm realistic, and I think he's sufficiently obsessed to do something stupid, yes.' He went over to her window and screwed tight the safety locks at each side. Donna sat down on the bed, and he added: 'You look pale.' He sat beside her and put his arm round her.

'I've had quite a few shocks over the last day or two,' she answered.

'So you have.' His arm was warm, it comforted her. She moved slightly, remembering all that had happened, remembering Laura.

'Relax,' he said. 'Shall I get you something to drink? A drop of brandy?'

'I don't know.' Her emotional defences were at a

low ebb, she felt childlike and afraid, and she wanted him to continue holding her, and that was wrong.

'Get yourself ready for bed. I'll go and put the alarm on. I'll bring you a drink back.' Brent stood up, gave her a brief look that seemed to hold more understanding than his words had shown, and went out. Donna went in to have a shower. Her body ached with exhaustion, and she felt emotionally drained. She ran the cool water—fresh, not from the sea, a blissful difference, and the cool spray refreshed her slightly. Then she walked slowly back and eased herself into bed, and lay down.

He came in silently, holding a glass with a small measure of golden liquid inside, said: 'Sit up Donna,' and she did so, obedient as the child she felt herself to be. He saw. He saw too much, for he added: 'Do you want me to stay?'

No! she thought, on an inward catch of breath, then—yes. 'I don't know,' she said in a small voice. 'No—I——'

'Just to stay, to be near you, that's all.'

Her mouth twisted involuntarily, she wanted to weep, and she didn't want him to see—and he added, in words that would remain with her for ever: 'I'm a guest under Nonie's roof. There's no way I would abuse her hospitality, Donna,' and she looked up and saw the truth of his words shining in his eyes, and she nodded.

'Would you? I am afraid.'

He took her hand. 'I know. I'm sorry, I shouldn't have told you. I'm almost positive there'll be no trouble. I am, as you so rightly said, probably being over-cautious. And I wouldn't have told you anything yet if you hadn't been so aware of my concern, and asked.'

He went and switched the light off, came back, said: 'Move over, I'll lie on top of the sheet,' then lay beside her. She moved back, inch by inch until there was room for him, and he leaned on his side, put his arm round her and said: 'Now, sleep. And in the morning I'll go and see Steven at his hotel—and you won't be bothered with him again.'

'How—how do you know where he is?'

'Because, my beautiful idiot, he'd left his phone number so that he could be contacted by the plane hire firm when you arrived. I—er—persuaded them to let me have it, and also to delay telling him for a day.' He smiled softly. 'I couldn't, however, be entirely sure they were to be trusted, hence the caution. But tomorrow, and after, you'll be free.'

'Why didn't you tell me this before?'

'I had to be sure you agreed to our "engagement" first. And you weren't ready to hear it all. You looked as though someone had hit you hard, out there on the terrace, Donna. I only told you what was essential.'

She was silent after his words, digesting them, knowing what truth there was—and concern—behind them. She felt protected, his caring cloaking her in a warm blanket, and she gave a little murmur and moved her hand to touch his cheek. 'Thank you,' she whispered. 'You're a wonderful man, Brent.'

'You'll make me blush in a minute if you say things like that!' He seemed amused, no more than that, and Donna cringed at her naïvety. Brent didn't want words like that from her. He didn't need them, or her, or anybody.

'I'm sorry.' The words were out even as thought.

'Don't apologise, I wasn't laughing at you, cuckoo. I was just thinking what an effect the brandy must have had.'

'That's not the brandy talking, it's me. I love you.' God! What had she *done*? She froze, horrified. *She hadn't intended to say that!*

'Say that again.'

'No! I—I'm drunk,' she said wildly, twisting away, panic-stricken.

'You said you loved me.' Brent held her, caught her tightly, stopped her escape.

'I don't know what made me say it,' she gasped. 'Truly—I'm——'

'Did you mean it, Donna?' He sat up, pulling her with him, and she cried out in pain.

'I—let me go, please—my foot——' but he held her, ignored her pleas. 'I—yes, yes, all right, *yes*—I *did*—let me go!'

He did. He released her, sat up, leaned forward, and put his hands to his head. Trembling, she said: 'Perhaps you'd better go, Brent.' Scarcely were the words out of her mouth then he turned, put his arms round her, and kissed her, a long deep soul-searching kiss that made her see stars for a few seconds. And when it was over he gave a long shuddering sigh, and said: 'And I love you—very much.'

He was cruel doing that. She made a murmur of pain, deep in her throat, and shook her head. 'Don't please,' she said weakly.

'Don't tell you?' He kissed her again and again, wonderful, warm, *loving* kisses. 'Do you want me to *prove* it?'

She clung to him, laughing and crying at the same

time, caught up in the wonder of it, of him—knowing now, realising at last the truth. They held each other tightly as if they would never be able to let go of each other, lost in mutual wonder, feeling the warmth of desire, knowing too their unspoken promise to Nonie, the rules that made lovemaking impossible. But they could kiss, and did, could touch, and did, until eventually, shaking like a leaf, Brent pulled himself away and said huskily: 'I'd better take a cold shower.'

Donna pulled him back, and he didn't resist, and the next few minutes were lost in their mutual desire, and need. Until—he managed, desperately, to hold himself back from her, stagger into the bathroom, and run the shower strongly, the water drenching him. She saw him through the open door, watched him get out, shake himself and grab a towel. Then, putting his trousers on again, he came out, rubbing his hair and said, with a deep sad sigh: 'That's better. No, not better—but it's cooled me down.' He sat primly on the end of the bed, still rubbing his hair.

'Can we make the engagement real?' he said.

Donna smiled to herself. 'I thought you'd never ask!' He flung the towel down on the floor and said, his voice quieter:

'Donna, sit up, will you? I daren't lie down again— not just yet.' She sat up, hugging her knees, and he caught one of her hands and pressed it to his lips. 'There's something I have to tell you,' he said. And she knew what was to come, and said quietly:

'I think I know what it is.'

'About—Laura?'

'Yes—Nonie told me. Brent, you don't need to— I——'

'Yes, I do. I thought Nonie might have. But she doesn't know the full story.'

'It doesn't matter,' she said very quietly. 'I love you so deeply—I felt pain when Nonie told me—about her—but that's gone. Even if you always love Laura, and remember her, I'll—understand.'

'No, you won't. Not until you know the truth. Because you see, I suspect that Nonie will have also told you how alike you and Laura are.' Her silence answered him and he went on: 'I thought so. And you—you must have thought——' he paused, and it was evident that he was searching for the words. She wanted to help him, wanted to take him to her, but she knew she must not. He had to say what he needed to. She held his hand tightly, letting him know, giving him her strength, for she sensed *his* pain. 'You must have thought, when I was making love to you, that——' the words were not coming easily. 'That I was perhaps thinking of her. Did you?'

Donna could not lie. 'Yes,' she said.

He took a deep breath. 'Thank you. I did love Laura once, very much. She was a bright, golden girl, a wonderful person—so I thought, and that was the girl I fell for, hook, line and sinker. I thought she loved me equally—she never gave me any cause to doubt it—and I was about to ask her to marry me, had bought the ring, planned a surprise party, the lot—when a "friend"——' the word was tinged with irony, 'told me that she was faithless, I don't mean in the sense that she'd cheated on me, seen another man when I was away—I could have forgiven that—but that she was utterly and totally amoral, always had been, always would be. I hit him—hard. That was the last time I ever struck anyone—and probably the reason I now deplore violence—because what he had told me was true, as I found out the days following, tackled her with it, and she looked at me, with her sweet, beautiful face, and told me that she could never be faithful to one man, that *that* was the way she was, and if I didn't like it, I knew what I could do. I walked out on her and never saw her again. And from that day on I never fell in love. I had affairs, where we both knew the score at the beginning, and no commitment was expected on either side. I was, I suppose, very bitter, thinking that I still loved her, and had been badly treated. Then she was killed. I knew then that what I'd felt those years in between was sheer, selfish self-pity. I went to her funeral, and said my goodbyes, and in my heart, I forgave her. For she was like a bright butterfly, as conscienceless as that, beautiful and devastating in her effect. And I was free.' He paused, and Donna took his hand, and kissed it, and he smiled, and touched her cheek gently.

'When we met, I was reminded forcefully of Laura, not unnaturally, and I saw in you the selfishness she possessed, all the faults—none of the good, the wonderful bright side of her I'd once known. Until— very soon, you changed. And the night you told me about the terrible thing you'd suffered when you were twelve, opened my eyes to so many things—I can't even begin to tell you—but it was as if I'd been shocked out of my confidence in *my* rightness in everything.' He squeezed her hand.

'You began to teach *me*—to change me.' He kissed her, a light gentle kiss. 'I suppose, the night you made that dinner on deck—was it only *three* nights ago?' He laughed. 'It seems a lifetime! I suppose that was when

I really looked at you properly for the first time. You'd created something far beyond what you intended, and I looked at you, and saw *you* for the first time, and knew I loved you. It hit me as quickly and simply as that.'

'And I made it a special meal—and it had an added ingredient I hadn't thought you'd be aware of,' said Donna. 'I put love into it. Every tiny part of it was with my love.'

'I know. I know, my darling.'

'When I fell, and you carried me down to your cabin—I seemed to see a smile on your face, and it puzzled me. I think I know why, now.'

'Did I smile? How cruel you must have thought me! Of course I did! It saved me having to use any subterfuge. I now had a legitimate reason for taking you to your godmother—who at that stage I had no idea was Nemone.' He began to laugh. 'When you described her house I nearly fainted with shock! How I managed to keep my face straight I don't know.'

'I think she knew you'd be there when she told *me* to go,' said Donna. 'I don't know how, but I'm sure she knew.'

'So am I,' he agreed. 'And we'll find out, one way or another. And now, dearest heart, *I* am going to sleep on the floor. There's no way I will sleep on your bed with you in reach. So I'm going to drag my mattress in and——'

'There's no need,' she interrupted. 'Really, I'm not frightened of anything now. You can sleep in your own bed——'

'Until I can get a special licence,' murmured Brent, and kissed her. 'And if Nonie doesn't mind, how do you feel about spending at least a part of your honeymoon here?'

'Lovely. As for Nonie *minding*—don't you think she might have already planned it that way?'

'I wouldn't be at all surprised. She said she was tired tonight, and went to bed early. Come to think of it, she looked more wide awake than we did. Tired! She's probably sitting up in bed planning her wedding outfit.'

'Shall we go and see? Go and tell her?' Donna giggled.

'Let's creep along and see if her light is on.' Hand in hand, they padded out, past the hall, along the passage to Nonie's room. The light under the door was evidence enough. They glanced at each other, then Brent tapped the door, and a very wide-awake voice said:

'Come in.'

Nonie was sitting up in bed, a large book on her knee. She peered over her reading glasses, took them off, and said brightly: 'Come and sit down, my dears. What a nice surprise.' She didn't seem at all surprised. Complacent would be a better word, thought Donna.

'You knew, didn't you?' said Donna.

'Knew what, my dears?' Bright innocence personified.

'That Brent would be on the island when *you* sent me there?'

There was a brief pregnant silence, then: 'Ah! Hadn't you better sit down?'

They did so, and Brent leaned forward and kissed the old woman's cheek. 'And after you've confessed *all*,' he told her, 'we have something extremely interesting to tell *you*.'

'Well,' said Nonie, 'in *that* case. It's like this, you see. I happened to be on the phone to your father one day, just a couple of weeks ago, and——'

Donna and Brent exchanged knowing glances. This could take a time. They could wait. They had all the time in the world. A lifetime, in fact.

Coming Next Month in Harlequin Romances!

2665 PETER'S SISTER Jeanne Allan
A battle-scarred Vietnam veteran shows up in Colorado and triggers painful memories in his buddy's sister. He reminds her of the brother she lost and the love she's never forgotten.

2666 ONCE FOR ALL TIME Betty Neels
When tragedy strikes a London nurse, support comes — not from her fiancé — but from her supervising doctor. But she finds little comfort, knowing he's already involved with another woman.

2667 DARKER FIRE Morgan Patterson
Because she so desperately needs the job, a Denver secretary lies about her marital status. But how can she disguise her feelings when her boss asks her to leave her husband and marry him instead?

2668 CHÂTEAU VILLON Emily Spenser
Her wealthy French grandfather tries to make amends for having disinherited her father. Instead, he alienates Camille and the winery's heir when he forces them to marry before love has a chance to take root.

2669 TORMENTED RHAPSODY Nicola West
The idea of returning to the tiny Scottish village of her childhood tantalizes and torments a young Englishwoman. Inevitably, she'll run into the man who once broke her heart with his indifference.

2670 CATCH A FALLING STAR Rena Young
Everyone in the music business calls her the Ice Maiden. But there's one man in Australia capable of melting her reserve — if only to sign her with his nearly bankrupt recording company.

Introducing

Harlequin Intrigue

Because romance can be quite an adventure.

Available in August wherever paperbacks are sold.

INT-3

4 FREE
Harlequin Romances